New Girl in Town

Also Available in Large Print
by Faith Baldwin

Time and the Hour

New Girl in Town

FAITH BALDWIN

Faith Baldwin Cuthrell

G.K.HALL &CO.

GKH Boston, Massachusetts

1975

Library of Congress Cataloging in Publication Data

Cuthrell, Faith Baldwin, 1893 -
  New girl in town.

  Large print ed.
  1. Sight-saving books. I. Title.
[PZ3.C973Ne3]   [PS3505.U97]   813'.5'2   75-19485
ISBN 0-8161-6305-7

Published in Large Print by arrangement with Holt, Rinehart and Winston

Set in Photon 18 pt Crown

I dedicate this book to the men in my life
in the order of their appearance:
Bruce,
Stephen,
John,
Chet,
Ray,
David,
Walter,
and Bill
And, of course, to the women in theirs.

PREFACE

The first Little Oxford book was published in 1939 — a collection of six connected novelettes. The second was in 1971. Because I wished to write a story of imaginary ex-urban life, and was too lazy to invent a name, I then remembered *Station Wagon Set* and reread it. So I had a name, and also characters who would probably still be alive. Since then, there have been Little Oxford books in 1973 and 1974.

In none is stated the exact year, but they are, I think, sufficiently contemporary. This one I began just as the cold shadow of the energy crisis fell upon us. It had been coming for years, but few realized it. There were wars, aftermaths of wars and political confusions. I have not written of these. Up-to-the-hour novels are being, and will be, written every day; also nonfiction. I am a storyteller, not a historian or a critic, for which I apologize.

Faith Baldwin

Norwalk, Connecticut
February 13, 1974

New Girl in Town

1

The new girl in Little Oxford was Margaret Knox, usually called Maggie. Early in November she had been the houseguest of Letty Irvington and her physician husband, Benjamin, always called Bing. On that particular evening they were giving a buffet supper to present her, as Bing remarked, at the Court of St. James's.

Maggie was young and there were young people at the Irvingtons', some of whom she'd met during her few days there — Katie and Jeremy Palmer; Amy and Ben Irvington, who practiced with his father; Stacy and Lee Osborne — and older people also, such as Gordon Banks, the handsome, recently retired clergyman, and his beautiful wife; and even Bing's old friend and patient, Rosie Niles, who was up from town for the night.

During the evening, guests shuttled between the living room, where the buffet and bar were presided over by the Irvingtons' Priceless Pearl and some outside help, and Bing's fire-lighted study — a mishmash of order and disorder which looked, and was, lived in. Oscar, the beagle bought for his son but living mostly with Bing, was there also.

Letty Irvington drifted into the study and inquired, "Has everyone had enough to eat?" Happy groans replied and she said, "Pearl and Company will bring in coffee and Scotch, plates and glasses. Looks like a convention of redheads in here."

Her own hair was silver-gilt and Bing spoke to Maggie: "Welcome to the Club. Letty's not a member."

"Pop's President," Ben Irvington said, regarding his parent with favor. "I'm next in line."

Bing's hair was old Sheffield, silver on copper. He patted the top of his daughter-in-law's head and suggested, "I think Amy's can qualify in certain lights."

"Mine's chestnut," said Amy, "much more unusual."

"Me," said Maggie sadly, "I'm plain red."

Her hair was also short, thick and held an untamed wave, courtesy of Nature, which had also provided bright-blue eyes, a few freckles to accent what looked like a permanently tanned skin, and a slightly snub nose.

"You inherit your coloring from your grandaunt," Bing told her. "When I first came home to practice with my father, Hattie came to see me — her own doctor being away, she explained. She didn't approve of my father taking a vacation, sick leave or seminar. She looked me up and down and she was not much shorter than I. 'Redheaded brat,' she said, and I retorted, 'Look who's talking.' I was seared by the old-fashioned look she gave me. She was somewhat my senior. Rachel — your mother — was dark. Did you know Letty and I were at her wedding? I never saw her again. Nor your father, of course."

"I never saw him either."

"I know. Hattie flew to California when you were born and then had to tell Rachel

3

that her young husband had been killed in Korea. She told me, when she returned, that it was the hardest thing she'd ever had to do. She wanted to bring you both back with her."

Letty said, "I wonder why Rachel didn't want to come. Hattie raised her."

"I think because she and my father lived their brief months together in California; also she worked there."

"Rachel," Bing explained to the others, "was a very capable graduate of our hospital. She met Maggie's father — who was from Deeport — on his last leave home. I hadn't known him. . . . Are there any relatives?" he asked Maggie.

"I don't believe so. His parents died in a flu epidemic. Aunt Hattie told me that. Perhaps there are cousins. I'll ask Mr. Comstock; he might know. Aunt Hattie came out to California when mother remarried and, later, several times to Hawaii. After my mother died in the car accident, Aunt Hattie wanted me to come east and live with her. I loved her, but I couldn't. Greg — Gregory Knox, my stepfather — had adopted me as soon as he could after we went to the Islands. Before my mother's death, he was manager on a plantation — I was in Honolulu, studying to be a medical secretary; Lani, my stepsister — really my sister, I feel — was in North Carolina at the University. When she graduated, she took over the job of hostess a great deal better than I. I just played at it. Lani was born to be a diplomat's wife. On a plantation of that size the entertaining, whether compulsory or not, is tremendous. Anyway, once Lani was in charge, I went back to California, where I worked and shared an apartment with a girl I knew from Hilo."

"How about your possessions," Letty asked, "now that you've decided to give New England a chance?"

"I don't own much." Maggie smiled, and when she did, the sun came out for anyone looking at her. "I wouldn't want furniture from the plantation, not even my mother's. Too unsuitable. Greg will send on things I cherish from childhood, however much he disapproves of my staying on here. I don't have anything in Vi's apartment except clothes and some trinkets. Mother's jewelry — Greg gave it to her — is in a Honolulu bank. Vi can send me the California clothes, but for cold weather here I'll certainly have to buy a new wardrobe." She paused as Jeremy Palmer and his wife came from the living room.

Jeremy, long, lean and somewhat stooping, said, "We eavesdropped. I hope you have a lot of books, valuable books and will have them sent here and also that you'll have no idea how much they're worth. I would then offer you what I consider to be a fair price, Maggie."

His wife, at his heels, cried, "Don't listen to him. He charms, then cheats."

"I'm not much of a reader," Maggie told Jeremy. "All I'll have sent here are a few of my favorite paperbacks, mostly science fiction." She added, "And some dictionaries and medical textbooks."

Jeremy said, staggered, "A deathblow to a bookseller. The gal doesn't read much and is not, I daresay, a patroness of the lending library. I suggest she be cast out of Eden."

Stacy Osborne, sitting near Maggie,

said, "Are you intimidated? I was for a time, by the town, as a bona fide newcomer. I'd only heard of Little Oxford. Your mother, your grandaunt, your mother's parents were all born here, your father nearby.You're even a distant relative, I understand, of Bing's. You've got it made, Maggie. I was terrified of this place. My only friends were Lee's sister and Vanessa."

"What about me?" Lee asked.

"I didn't even like you," said Stacy and Maggie asked, laughing, "Who's Vanessa? She sounds out of Hugh Walpole."

"So you do read after all," said Jeremy reproachfully.

"I just said, 'Not much. . . .' Who is she?"

"Our local witch, complete with familiar," Ben answered. "You'll meet her. Stacy can brief you."

The party began to splinter off with cries of "Dear heaven, the baby-sitter will have eaten us out of house and home." Also, "You must come to our house, and I'm dying to see yours. I was never inside the old Holton place."

7

Maggie collapsed in a large chair and Oscar came to lie at her feet. "Marvelous people!" she said. "I'm so grateful to you both. It's like being in the Islands — not in the touristy parts."

"Not everyone here is a native nobleman," Bing warned her, smiling.

"I do wish," Maggie said sadly, "I had some of Aunt Hattie's dignity. I'm too small. I'm too grasshopper. Greg says I'm like a puppy, wagging its tail at everyone. I suppose that sounds worse than when he first said it," she reflected. "I tried platform shoes, but I kept falling down. My podiatrist got tired of seeing me limp into the office."

It irked Maggie not to have what her grandaunt had, called "presence." She weighed under one hundred pounds even after a tremendous *luau* or an eight-course banquet. She ate like a bird, in that she, as birds do, ate a great deal (most people don't realize this) and rarely gained an ounce. (Birds don't either.)

"You're fond of your stepfather," Bing surmised.

"Only father I ever knew and tops. He

was a widower — oh, you know that — when he came briefly to the mainland — well it used to be called that — met, fell in love with and married mother. He had a little girl about my age — I was three. We hated each other on sight, Lani and I, but in six weeks were fast friends. I missed her when she went to Chapel Hill. I miss her right now. . . . Dr. Bing, I need a job!"

He began, mildly surprised, "But your Aunt Hattie — "

"Left me everything. I know. She changed her will when Mother died. The house, the furniture, the land — two acres — the car . . . I didn't take mine to California. Now Greg will sell it for me or buy it for Lani. I wanted to give it to her, but he said I was always impractical."

"But there must be an income — " Bing began.

"Well, sure. Aunt Hattie brought Mother up after the epidemic — she spoiled her and me too — but she saw to it that Mother had a profession. I know. Aunt Hattie was always thrifty and had sound investments and that the antique shop brought a good price. Mr. Comstock told me."

"Excellent," Bing agreed. "Emily Warner sold it — she's Katie Palmer's boss — but every so often Hattie bought and fell in love with something, so it's in the house, and was never in the shop."

"I'm trained to slavery," said Maggie, "and I'd go nuts not working. I'd be restless on a cushion and can't sew any kind of seam, let alone a fine one. Maybe there'd be something for me at the hospital. . . . Besides, a girl can always use a little more money. The estate won't be settled for a while. Mr. Comstock says he'll advance me anything I need, and I had some savings after a year or so of work, not much — I'm wildly extravagant — and Greg said to phone him if I want anything."

"Phone!" said Letty horrified. Her idea of long distance was California where the Irvingtons' daughter lived with her husband and children.

"Of course," said Maggie. "I called Greg from the motel after figuring out time differences, and before you rescued

10

me from that impersonal room which smelled of salesmen — clean salesmen." she interpolated earnestly, "and from taxis at exorbitant rates and the feeling of being on another planet."

Letty remembered scooping Maggie up at Bing's request and how defenseless she had looked at her grandaunt's funeral services. She said gently, "You're half-asleep; go to bed. Tomorrow's your big day. . . . Katie's helping, isn't she?"

"Oh yes, but I think everything's been done. Mr. Comstock had the house cleaned — all I have to do is get settled. . . . Do you think it will snow soon?"

"Not for a while. Usually not before Thanksgiving, although it's been known. Are you scared?" Letty asked.

"I've seen snow only in pictures, movies, paintings and on mountains," Maggie said, "and I've wondered why no one's figured out how to make it stop."

There was a silence. "She's asleep," said Letty. "Bring her along upstairs."

As Bing lifted her, she sighed and said something he didn't hear. He carried her up, following Letty, who opened a guest-room door, and gave orders. "Put her down. No, silly, on the bed. I'll take over. See you later, darling."

She looked at Maggie, and said aloud, "I hope the little thing will like it here."

"I do," said Maggie, indignantly sitting upright. "And there you go! You're not so big yourself." She added, "How'd I get here?"

"Bing," said his wife. "He's used to toting little girls. He has had a daughter; now he has her little girls. He's also had Ben and Ben's child."

"I think it's wonderful here," said Maggie, not far from tears.

"You'll learn the language," Letty told her, "and adapt to the customs of the natives. Do get undressed, Maggie, and go to sleep; you've had a long evening. If you need something to help, I'll ask Bing, though he won't approve."

"I don't need anything," said Maggie, with her heartwarming smile. "You're wonderful too."

A little later, asleep under an electric blanket — Letty's instructions, as the night was sharp — she was dreaming of another time and another place, a different breeze, a bigger moon and stars. She was dreaming of a man with whom she had once been slightly in love and of fields of sugarcane, and of snow-topped mountains seen through the violet-blue haze of jacaranda trees.

It was a curious experience, going into the Holton house the next morning. Maggie had been there briefly with Andrew Comstock, her aunt's lawyer — now hers — a big, quiet man whom she liked very much. But while she'd known the house belonged to her — as did the clean, well-kept, three-year-old car in the garage, and the space surrounding the old structure — it had all seemed unreal. She'd seen snapshots which Hattie had sent and her mother had had an old album filled with pictures of the house and of herself, from childhood to her wedding. But today, walking in with Katie, Maggie had a different feeling entirely.

Empty, dusted, and with shades drawn, the house waited patiently as it had for a century and a half, maybe more, Mr.

13

Comstock had said.

Once a small farmhouse, it had had Civil War porches, but Aunt Hattie had scrapped them — her parents would have been horrified, she'd said once; perhaps they even were — and had layers of old paint removed from the wide random board floors. She had kept the house in excellent condition. A buyer who fancied an old house with two acres within walking distance of town could have marched in, sat down and felt at home. Mr. Comstock had told Maggie that the house would command a splendid price. The acreage alone was valuable, and if she wished to sell the furniture, the sky would be more or less the limit. He was a man who liked old furniture and old houses. "I might even make a bid for something," he said. "My insensitive son, on the other hand, prefers modernity — in everything."

Maggie hadn't met Matthew Comstock. He was, she understood, trying a case somewhere in the state. At the Capitol perhaps? She was extremely hazy on the subject of law. Fortunately, she trusted the older partner, Andrew, as her aunt had before her, and obediently signed the papers he placed before her, and listened with respect to his careful explanations.

"Good heavens!" said Katie, hauling a couple of bags, as Maggie searched for, and found, the house key. "Do hurry. I'm dying to get my foot in the door, and what a beautiful door!"

Maggie said, "Hey, gimme that bag. I was so sort of dazed I didn't realize you'd taken it."

Two pieces of luggage, not weighing much.

They went in and put the bags down — the suitcase, the flight bag — and Katie started raising the shades. "Heavenly days," she said in awe, "will you look at the stuff she — you — have!"

"Katie, Aunt Hattie had an antique shop."

"I know. I was in it before she sold it. I couldn't cope with the prices, and I hear they're worse now. Jeremy cries a lot when he goes in. He's hooked on antiques — has some himself. Maggie, if you do decide to sell, swear to me on whatever you hold dear — your honor, your virtue, your chance of salvation — that you'll let Warner and Associates handle it."

"I promise," said Maggie, touching a beautiful Pembroke table, then crossing the living room to a desk. "I wonder where this came from."

''Perhaps some ancestral schoolteacher," said Katie, "during the Revolution. I don't really know. Jeremy has books. He'll lend them to you. Also he'll come and look, expound and beg you, if you wish to sell anything — after all it's somewhat busy in this room, isn't it? — to give him first choice. Be very careful if you do."

The curtains were embroidered crewel, with a scatter of flowers, rose, pale green, a hint of sunny yellow, and Maggie said, "I remember Aunt Hattie wrote that she was making these, after she sold the shop."

There was a fireplace with a handsome old mantel and old andirons; there were chairs, some with petit point; there were hassocks; a good many windows so that even on a graying November day there seemed to be sun.

The lamps were old glass, old china, and electrified. The end of the living room which was next to the kitchen widened to accommodate a harvest table, comfortable Windsor chairs, and a serving table. The kitchen itself was big and completely modern. "I remember when Aunt Hattie decided to do it over," Maggie said. "She was in Hawaii with us and said that just because her ancestors cooked in the fireplace, and also froze to death, she saw no reason why she should."

Living room, dining area, kitchen, a powder room and the short square hall downstairs. Upstairs — and they were narrow stairs and steep — a bathroom and three bedrooms, one with a stall shower.

"She had that done for me," Maggie said — and her eyes stung — "when she thought I might come to live with her."

The walls were papered, the beds were old — two were four-posters; in the third bedroom, a gooseneck.

"It will take months for me to get used to this," Maggie said. "Well . . . let's see what we need from the store."

In the kitchen cabinets, all the staples

and in the freezer, frozen foods. The refrigerator had been cleaned out.

"Damned little," said Katie. "Milk, cream, eggs, butter or whatever you use. I'm a terrible cook. Jeremy's fabulous. You must come to dinner very soon. He'll cook up a storm for you if you'll let him go through this house and brood."

"I can cook," Maggie said, "and I hope you'll both come here often. Bring offspring. We'll put him to bed. . . . For heaven's sake! I just remembered Mr. Comstock's saying there were things in the attic. We haven't been up there. You haul down a ladder — from the hallway ceiling, I think. Anyway he said homemade things, a rocking horse, a crib. . . . I'm starved."

"I suppose I'll get used to the way you abrubtly change the subject," said Katie.

"Grasshopper genes."

"We can have a sandwich or salad downtown."

"I'd rather have something here. First, I'm going to turn on the heat. There must be a thermostat."

"It's on," said Katie. "I'm warm. What's the matter? You delicate?"

"No, but Southern California and the Islands have thinned my blood, I guess," Maggie said apologetically. "All right, we can eat downtown, though I'd rather fix lunch."

"You can really cook?"

"Of course. But I'm not orderly. This house is though. I'll have to ask Mr. Comstock if I can afford someone to clean — say, once a week. I shudder to think of the grass next summer and I don't know much about your kind of flowers."

"Flowers are cousins wherever they come from. They love sun, rain, freedom from weeds. That's all they need."

"So you garden?"

"Very little," Katie admitted cheerfully. "Come on, let's go."

When they returned, she wouldn't come in. She said, "You'll manage. Call if you need us. Come to dinner day after tomorrow. Jeremy will pick you up."

"I'll call Mr. Comstock," said Maggie. "Thanks for everything." She hugged Katie, adding, "I think I'm going to like it here."

But when she heard Katie's car drive away, she felt forlorn and abandoned. She walked slowly around the living room looking from the windows, looking at the bookcases. Hattie Holton had had a great many books. They were here, in the wide upstairs hall, and in the bedrooms. She must make up her mind which bedroom would be hers. Mr. Comstock had recommended the southwest corner room. "Your grandaunt's," he'd said.

Maggie went upstairs and into the room. She looked in the closets. Aunt Hattie's clothes were there and, in the tallboy and lowboy, handkerchiefs, underwear, stockings. There were shoes in a small built-in cupboard. And Maggie said aloud, "Maybe I'd better go back to the motel."

But the other rooms were empty of personality. She'd take the one next door which had been, she thought, her mother's.

There was a telephone in the downstairs hall and an extension in Hattie's room. Returning there, Maggie sat down on the big canopied bed and dialed Comstock and Comstock. Reaching the secretary, she asked if she could have an appointment that afternoon or the following day.

Mrs. Daniels replied that Mr. Comstock was out of town but that Mr. Matt Comstock would be in the office tomorrow.

So Maggie could see him at two o'clock. That would be the partner who likes "everything modern." He must hate the house, thought Maggie, but I'm contemporary.

2

Shortly after Maggie had unpacked her few belongings and stashed them away, she went downstairs to make herself a cup of tea. She'd stopped with Katie, on the way home, to get coffee, milk, and a few other items at one of the markets. Sitting in the rocking chair in the kitchen, she observed Hattie's houseplants — geraniums here on the windowsill. Apparently they had been watered not long ago.

The telephone spoke and Maggie ran into the hall to answer. It was Letty Irvington saying, "I called before. No one home."

"Katie and I went out and had some lunch, and did a little shopping. Actually, I'd hardly anything to buy."

"I know." Letty reflected that Hattie, a woman who had moved quickly and silently, had died in a like manner, causing no unnecessary fuss, speculation or delay. "Lonely?"

"Well, a little. Now, about someone to clean . . . that is, unless this house is self-cleaning like an oven — incidentally, there's one here, very new."

"Mrs. Green," said Letty promptly. "She comes in sometimes to help Pearl. She knows the house. Your aunt had her. She's capable and reliable. She doesn't gossip. Oh, she'll tell you what's going on, but that's different. I'll give you her number. Want me to come get you for supper? Bing's going to a dinner — hospital business."

"I'd love to," said Maggie truthfully, "but I can't."

"Someone holding you against your will or are you afraid of breaking a law?"

"I should have said 'mustn't.' I have to get used to being alone. I never have been," Maggie said.

"All right. Suppose I drop by after we've both had supper and make some suggestions?"

When Letty came, Maggie was watching TV — there was a small, good color set in Hattie's bedroom — so she didn't hear the bell. As the door was unlocked, Letty marched in and made inquiry.

"Maggie?"

Maggie came flying downstairs. She said, "I was watching TV . . . took me a while to get used to the stations at the motel and in your house. Aunt Hattie had a set in her bedroom."

"She wouldn't have it in the living room. She said it ruined conversations when guests came and she'd rather have conversations than television. She told us once that practically everyone she knew was so addicted that when they came into a house they made a beeline for the set. She said she used hers when alone or when she couldn't sleep, or if there was something worthwhile. . . . You shouldn't leave your front — or back — door open, Maggie," Letty said.

"I haven't really looked much out back. There's a sort of little stone porch and beyond that I guess you'd call it a summer patio."

Letty said, "Get used to the back porch — milkman, trashman, stray dogs, cats, raccoons, skunks or whatever's around."

"In a town!"

"Little Oxford isn't that much of a town."

"Then why should I lock doors? I know you have to to in cities, even in the Islands — "

"Things change. When I was born right in this village, no one locked doors. Maggie, after you're settled perhaps we can help you find a nice compatible working girl — a teacher or nurse perhaps — who'd like to have that smaller room and shower deal, perhaps cooking privileges, and pay enough to help with expenses."

"I'd hate it!"

"But you said you shared an apartment in California."

"With Vi. Oh, yes, I'd known her since we were kids. Love her a lot too, but I couldn't stand her when we shared the flat. We had dates at the wrong times; she wanted me out when I'd rather be in and vice versa. We had a couple of fights — she had red hair too, more auburn — over a man. He was a pilot and didn't, I think, give a hoot for either of us. We thought he was marvelous. There's something about pilots. . . . Do you like music, Mrs. Irvington?"

"Letty to you as to everyone, including our grandchildren. . . . Yes. Why?"

"I have a small transistor with me, and there's one upstairs by Aunt Hattie's bed. I thought I'd make room for a stereo someday when I can afford it. I'd like to turn the smallest bedroom into a study. I could leave that beautiful gooseneck bed there, with lots of pillows on it and move the desk and the TV from Aunt Hattie's room in there. She had so much," Maggie said earnestly, "I could safely scatter it."

"I worry about you," Letty said.

"I'm not brave," Maggie admitted. "I've lived most of my life in a place without, for instance, snakes. I don't recall any on the streets of Los Angeles when I was a baby. But when I went back and Vi took me into the country — it was gorgeous as it happened to be in a season without mud slides, brush or forest fires, and no earthquakes — but I saw a snake. I'll never recover. I suppose," she asked resigned, "you have them here?"

"We certainly do," Letty said affably. "None, however, on most people's doorsteps."

"I'm seeing my lawyer tomorrow," Maggie announced with her usual abrupt change of subject.

Letty blinked. "Any special reason? Such as no trespassing by snakes?"

"Oh, about the car and whether I can afford a cleaning woman . . . your Mrs. Green. Aunt Hattie's Mrs. Green."

"Andrew Comstock's a very fine man," Letty said.

"I agree, but he's away. I'm to see the son."

"Matt?" Letty laughed. "You'll like him, I think."

"Why were you laughing?"

"Because I'm not sure. He's very unlike his father. He's mainly a trial lawyer. Very capable. Bing says he's wasted in this place. Personaly I think he has political ambitions."

"What's he really like?"

"A love-me-love-my-dog type."

"You mean — for real?"

"Yes, big dog. German shepherd. You

scared of dogs?''

"I'm not scared of dogs or horses — I can ride. I also swim, play tennis, some golf and soft ball. I'm not afraid of cats, birds or raccoons — I think I'd keep my distance from skunks — I'm just afraid of snakes, loud noises, fires and tidal waves.''

"You'll do,'' said Letty. "May I look around? I haven't been here for some time. I'd like to visualize what you propose to do with the third bedroom.''

Leaving, she advised, "Lock the doors and the downstairs windows, and get some sleep.''

Obediently, Maggie locked the front door after Letty's straight little back and turned off the light above it, went to the back door, put that light on and peered out. Something scampered in the bushes. As long as it didn't slither, she wished it luck. She locked that door too, turned out that light, darkened the living room and went upstairs to take a hot bath, find a book and read herself to sleep.

The guest room, which she hoped had been her mother's, was blue and white —

the bed wasn't canopied as was Aunt Hattie's — the furniture was mostly Victorian and very comfortable. And she'd found a comforter for the bed, which she could put over the sheets, blanket and patchwork quilt. On her shopping list there must be an electric blanket. She assumed Aunt Hattie would have scorned it but she was, she discovered the next day, mistaken. There were two on top of one of Aunt Hattie's closets. Boxed.

"Oh, Pioneer," Maggie said to herself.

The day was warm and sunny and she ate her very substantial breakfast to the music of someone named Jolly Roger. After which she decided to dress, walk to the shops, orient herself a little, and look in on Katie in the real estate office.

Yesterday Katie had said, "I got off by telling Mrs. Warner you could be a prospect. She really covets your house and despite a cautious — not to say lousy — market, my boss still manages to uncover big spenders. Now that I can leave my son and heir, I work full time. I want to. We have a very classy Mrs. Crane, an English-type nanny. She has a son in the city, and from her references she practically raised only minor royalty. I'm scared of what she'll do to our all-American boy. . . . By the way, you must meet Emily Warner. Those of us who work with her have been told we'll inherit the business. I dunno. But, in any case, she works me as hard as she did when I was childless.''

Now Maggie remembered this, smiling. She liked Katie and Amy. She felt she'd like Stacy if she came to know her, and she was close to loving Letty.

She thought: I'll have lunch at the place Katie took me to — The Checkered Tablecloth, wasn't it? — where they also make casseroles to take out — which is an idea if not too expensive. Anyway, they had great salads and sandwiches. I'll go early. There aren't many tables.

Maggie was usually hungry except when she was ill, or falling out of, or disappointed in, love.

Looking at her scanty wardrobe, she reflected that the clothes Vi had been asked to send wouldn't arrive for quite a while. Those she'd left at home would take even longer, but they wouldn't be suitable until summer anyway. Meantime, the black dress that she hoped never to wear again, the blue-and-white tweed suit, which she'd wear today, one pair of slacks and a shirt, and the in-between frock she'd worn to the party. She really would have to buy some clothes, she thought, making a few mental calculations. Perhaps Mr. Comstock would think clothes important — enough, that is, for an advance. He might, she thought further, unless he preferred nudist camps. He probably had a wife, daughter, daughter-in-law. She remembered distinctly that he himself had been very well clad when he met her plane and took her to the motel explaining, "I'm sorry, this is on the highway, but the Inn in Little Oxford is full up."

She walked downtown, looking at houses, speaking to dogs, children — two of whom nearly ran over her, one on a bicycle, the other on a three-wheeler. Now and then, someone smiled at her. She had a next-door neighbor but as yet had not seen her or him — or was it them? — and as Aunt

Hattie's house was on a corner, there was no one on the other side.

When she reached Colonial Way, she took her time, looking into the shop windows. Clothes, gifts, ice-cream parlors, pastry — everything seemed to be on these few blocks and she hadn't even seen the other side of the street except one of the markets to which Katie had taken her.

She went into Warner Associates and asked the girl, who seemed to be the receptionist, if Mrs. Palmer was in. "I'm Maggie Knox," she explained, "and Mrs. Palmer showed me around yesterday."

"I know," said Flo, the girl at the desk and telephone. "Welcome to Little Oxford, Miss Knox. I'm sorry Mrs. Palmer is out with a client. I don't know when she'll be back; she's to call in."

A door opened and Emily Warner emerged, a formidable woman, large, unadorned, majestic. There's "presence," thought Maggie, and Flo said, "It's Miss Knox, Mrs. Warner; she was looking for Katie."

Mrs. Warner extended a strong hand and

said, "We're glad you're here. Come into my office for a moment, will you?"

Maggie followed her in and was waved to a chair. Emily Warner regarded her with large, cool eyes. She said, "Katie's told me about you. She said you've decided to make your home here — "

"That's right — " Maggie began, but Mrs. Warner went on, " — in the Holton house. I've been in it a few times. Lovely old place. I knew your grandaunt fairly well, sold the shop for her. I knew your mother slightly. You look a little like her — and Hattie too. Katie says you'd be interested in a job. Ever consider real estate?"

She thought: Personality, a good speaking voice, not in the least bit nervous.

"No," said Maggie flatly. "I'd loathe it."

"Why?"

"I would probably want every attractive house I saw, and I don't know how to sell," said Maggie laughing. "I don't even *buy* with common sense."

"You could be trained," Emily suggested.

"I'm already trained as a medical secretary."

"Katie didn't tell me that. You're not interested in selling your house, are you — Maggie, isn't it?"

"Yes. I mean, yes, it's Maggie and no, I'm not interested in selling. For heaven's sake, I've only been there overnight."

"I know," said Emily. "But even with the market the way it is — apathetic, let's say, people afraid of spending and money very tight — there are still fortunate souls around who would pay an extravagant price for an old house in good condition — Hattie's was always kept in good condition — to say nothing of the furniture. I bought a few pieces from Hattie myself. We took some time bargaining over each one."

Maggie shook her red head. "Thanks just the same, but Dr. Irvington thinks he can get me work. I'll call Katie tonight." She rose and, smiling at Emily, said, "Come see the house anytime."

"And eat my heart out?" Emily inquired.

"Exactly," Maggie agreed sweetly and departed.

34

Emily liked people with spirit, which was one of the reasons why she was fond of Katie. When she was ready to retire — and she wasn't yet by a long shot — the business would belong to those associates who had been with her for some time, including Katie. She had no one else to leave it to. She could sell it and then retire, but she would not. She was without relatives and while she had many friends, few were close. She'd never had children.

Maggie marched herself into The Checkered Tablecloth with an excellent appetite. There was a table in the corner and she went toward it. There were others, but she liked corners. A pretty waitress gave her a menu — which was simple but more than adequate — and asked, "Weren't you here yesterday with Mrs. Palmer?"

"That's right. Thanks for remembering." Maggie glanced at the name embroidered on the apron bib and added, "Lois, I'd like the Chef Salad, the homemade rolls and lots of coffee."

The place soon filled up. There weren't more than seven or eight tables. The smell of casseroles in the oven was delicious. A very dark woman came in, looked around, conferred with a waitress and advanced upon Maggie. She said, "I met you at the Irvingtons'. I'm Rosie Niles. I didn't have much of a chance to talk to you and I had to leave early. May I sit with you?"

"Please," said Maggie. "I'd like it very much."

She remembered meeting Rosie Niles and asking Letty later who she was. "I thought you were just here for that evening," she said.

"Well, originally. . . . Lois, I'd like a very rare hamburger and milk." She turned back to Maggie. "I know hamburgers aren't on the menu, but the old-timers know they can always get them. Bing keeps howling at me to eat protein. . . . Yes, I intended to come up just for your party and spend one night at my own house and then drive back to the city. But one of the people who look after my place was ill and there was a crisis in an organization I'm interested in and a special meeting was called, so here I am. I'll go back this afternoon. How come you're here alone?''

"I'm to be at the Comstock office at two," Maggie said, looking at her watch. "I'm killing time."

"It often deserves to be murdered," Rosie said.

Maggie's order came and Rosie said, "I would have liked to drive you home. I haven't been in that house in years. Your grandaunt disapproved of me."

"I can't imagine why."

"Ask Letty or Bing or Ben," said Rosie. "Or I might even tell you myself someday. . . . Do you sing?''

"You're as bad as I am, Mrs. Niles," Maggie said, laughing. "Here's your hamburger."

"What do you mean bad as you are?''

"I grasshop — I mean, leap from one subject to the other."

"Oh, that! I daresay your old friends are used to it and the new ones will learn. . . . Well, do you sing?''

"Not a note, except in my head where I sing like Joan Sutherland, also Vikki Carr, Shirley Bassie and others. I'm a disgrace to Hawaii."

"Too bad," said Rosie. "It's fairly easy nowadays to find personality and a small voice. With mikes, that's all right. Personality and a great voice — that's not as simple. . . . I hate hamburgers," she remarked. "Also, I don't like milk. . . . However, I keep on looking and I spend considerable time trying to find kids who are worth giving training to here and in Europe. I've been lucky."

"They've been, you mean."

"No. I like doing something."

"Please, when you're here, come and see me."

"If Hattie Holton haunts the house — that's nice and alliterative — she'll push me downstairs."

"Then we needn't go upstairs. I hope she does haunt it. She was so good to my mother, and to me, and perhaps she doesn't disapprove of you now, Mrs. Niles."

"Rosie. . . . Why?"

"Oh, I dunno, but I think people have a different perspective when they leave this particular world for the next."

"I'd like to believe that," Rosie said.

"Tell me — I'm to see Mr. Andrew Comstock's son — what's he like?"

"Oh, sensational in his own way. I hope you like dogs."

"Yes. . . . Is he married?"

"No. He's looking, I expect, for the kind of wife who would help him to be governor or whatever he aims to be, although I think he'd be better off in an office or a courtroom. Maybe he wants the Supreme Court eventually. In any case, the right woman pushes and the wrong kind drags back."

"I can't stand politics," Maggie said, "and I know very little about it — or is it them?"

"Good. Tell Matt so sometime. Then he'll relax. It's common knowledge in Little Oxford that the attractive, intelligent girls who would like to be Mrs. Matthew Comstock attend political meetings, even get work on committees and read a lot. And it scares him. Or so his father, who is one of my lawyers, tells me."

The checks came, they paid them, tipped Lois and went out together.

"Remember," Maggie said, "you'll come see the house."

"Of course. Probably not until spring. I'm going to town for a spell and then to France. But I won't forget. Be happy here, Maggie. I think you have a great capacity for happiness."

Maggie walked on to the Comstock office. It was over a very elegant dress shop and boutique and she cautioned herself not to look into the shop windows. The office took up a whole floor. She remembered, of course, the reception room and also Mrs. Daniels, the secretary.

It was three minutes to two. The receptionist rang Mrs. Daniels, who appeared. "Good afternoon, Miss Knox. I'll take you in to see Mr. Matthew" — she smiled and explained — "we try to differentiate. He came in from lunch half an hour ago."

"Oh, I can find my way," Maggie said.

"Better not, the first time," Mrs. Daniels, who wouldn't see forty again and couldn't care less, said firmly.

3

Mrs. Daniels led a docile Maggie down the corridor past the senior partner's office and knocked at the next door.

Someone said, "Come in."

Mrs. Daniels opened the door, said, "Miss Knox," and departed.

A voice said firmly, "Sit."

Maggie thought: Where? She thought also that this was a peculiar way in which to greet a client — not so much as a "please," or "if you don't mind."

She looked across the room toward a large desk and the windows — the client always faces windows — and at the man who had risen and was advancing toward her. Then she saw the big police dog who had obeyed what she now realized had been a command. He was sitting. He did not, however, remove his beautiful, intelligent eyes from the stranger.

"You were talking to the dog," Maggie said. "Hi, Mr. Comstock. I thought you were talking to me."

"I don't bark at young women," Matt Comstock said, "or for that matter, at old ones. He doesn't either. Don't be nervous. Mrs. Daniels always accompanies new clients to the office, in case they are phobic. Didn't she warn you?"

"Not exactly, but other people already had — two to be specific."

He was now shaking her hand and smiling. He was tall, though not quite as tall as his father and did not resemble him. She thought: He's the best-looking homely man I ever saw, or is it the other way around?

She sat down in the chair he indicated and asked, "Would your dog — what's his name? — come over and make friends or is that verboten?"

"His AKC name is Baron Manfred Wolfgang Von *und zu* something. I've forgotten. His papers are in the safe. I thought of calling him Barry or Manny, Freddy or Wolfie. None seemed appropriate. So, he's called by, and answers to, the name of Moxie."

"Why?"

"Well, it's a slang term that's been around a long time. It's also the name of a soft drink, which is, I believe, still extant, and it means — in the argot anyway — courage — which is slightly more elegant than gutsy."

"His is a gutsy breed," Maggie commented and Matt regarded her with approval. He had eyes rather like Moxie's. "Say good afternoon to the lady, Moxie," he said.

Moxie rose and came over. Maggie sat perfectly still — it is tabu to make sudden gestures to a small child or an animal — and said, "Hi," softly.

Moxie put his elegant head on her knees.

She looked at Matt, now back behind his impressive desk. "Permission to pat?" she asked.

"Of course. You're accepted."

"He's beautifully marked, unusually so."

"You know something about shepherds, Miss Knox?"

"Oh, yes and a little about a number of

breeds. We've had lots of dogs at home."

"Hawaii?"

"Yes."

Moxie sighed, collapsed at her feet, and apparently fell asleep with one eye open.

"How old is he?"

"Four and a bit. I've had him since he was a pup, trained him to some degree and then sent him to obedience school. He goes where I do, with a few exceptions. I don't take him to anyone's house where there is a dog prejudice. Sometimes you don't know it until" — he smiled — "you ask for your first date . . . or to public entertainment . . . or to court where his appearance might sway some members of the jury. . . . Now, how can I help you in Dad's absence?"

She told him about the car and, hesitantly, about the money problem. "Not that it's urgent," she added. "I still have some cash and I'll transfer what funds I have in Los Angeles to a bank here. I'll need savings and checking accounts, wherever your father suggests."

"He'll suggest your grandaunt's bank. He's all for carrying on tradition."

"Aren't you?"

"Actually no, not exclusively. Why are you looking at me?"

"It's customary to look at the person who's speaking to you," Maggie said, "or is that too traditional?"

"I mean why are you looking at me in that particular way?"

"What way?"

He sighed, as Moxie had, except this was a sigh of exasperation. "Oh, as if I were being measured or checked up on — not exactly FBI or CIA, or police headquarters — but an appraisal perhaps, as if I'd applied for a loan or credit."

Maggie laughed. "Credit," she admitted and smiled at him. He had an undistinguished, battered sort of face — football, she thought, or was he born that way? — enlivened by bright dark eyes and squared off by a firm chin. Also topped by a shock of mouse-colored hair, not long, not too short and, she judged, in a state of continual dishevelment.

"What do you mean, credit?"

"On the personality scale," said Maggie.

"I won't ask my ratio. I'm a confirmed

coward. Are you always so candid?''

"I suppose so," she answered.

"Very like your grandaunt. One rather expected it of someone like Miss Hattie — if there ever was anyone like her. We live up the hill and to the left of you, so I'd turn up regularly at the house for cookies, milk and a frequent mild scolding. I was always dragging stray dogs and cats about, getting into poison ivy, scrambling over stone walls. She had a medicine cabinet for emergencies. I wasn't the only kid in the neighborhood.''

"Honesty is more becoming in someone who seems elderly to a small boy?''

"I dunno. Candid girls scare me. I haven't yet met many, but I never know if their candor is true or false. Like politicians.''

"I thought you wanted to be one.''

"May I ask who so informed you?''

"No.''

"Do you ever lie, Maggie Knox?" he asked.

"Certainly not.''

"Good God!" he said, staggered. Moxie's ears rose and he looked from his particular deity to Maggie.

"No one's perfect," Maggie said reproachfully. "Greg always told me I'd get into trouble sometime by not lying when called for."

"Your stepfather, I take it?"

"Yes. . . . Mr. Comstock, I've been here for practically hours and you haven't told me about the car, or the advance, if needed. Dr. Irvington thinks he can get me a job . . . the older Irvington, I mean."

"As a medical secretary? Shouldn't have too much difficulty."

"How do you know so much about me?"

"Dad has the dossier; we're partners," he said patiently. "What secrets we have from each other do not originate in the office." He had an engaging grin. Now he spoke in the intercom. "Any more appointments, Julia?" he asked. "Good. Mind the store, I'm shutting up my boutique. . . . Moxie and I will walk you home," he told Maggie. "I'll explain about the car as we go, but Dad will have to decide, as executor, how much will keep you from starvation."

"I can always call on Greg," said

Maggie. "I eat a lot."

"It doesn't show," said Matt.

Maggie mentally shook her red head. She liked Matt Comstock. This was unusual. As far as men were concerned, she had rules, also tendencies. She fell in love at once, or she took an instant dislike, or was wholly indifferent. She was drawn to older men because, she thought, of the father image, yet was turned off by married men.

Walking down Colonial Way and up Parsons Hill, she tried, but failed, to keep up with Matt's long lope. Moxie, however, endeavored to suit his paw steps to hers.

"Moxie, you're a very courteous person," Maggie said, "but I can't keep up with your Mr. Comstock."

"Call me Matt; I'm just a junior partner. I'm sorry — I'll slow down."

"You must be accustomed to long-legged girls."

"Yes, the tall athletic type usually. You, of course, are so diminutive, you must have to run to keep up with most of us."

"That's what you think," Maggie said. "Usually my escorts do moderate their pace physically," she explained. "What about the car?"

He explained the car situation, she listened, and they reached the house. Moxie appeared perfectly at home and Maggie judged he'd been here often.

Matt inquired, "Aren't you asking me in for milk and cookies?"

"Of course," Maggie said graciously. "What can I offer Moxie?"

"I'd allow him a healthy-type dog biscuit as a treat."

"Sorry, Moxie," Maggie told him, and he waved his tail tolerantly. "Next time I go shopping I'll remember, just in case you come again."

"He will. But you'll discover some in one of the cabinets," Matt said promptly. "Miss Hattie always kept them for him."

Maggie found her key and they went in.

"Hasn't changed," Matt remarked.

"I haven't had time," she said. Moxie walked about, sniffing, and finally marched into the kitchen and lay down, making a small but distinctly dismal sound.

"He knows," Matt told her. "Dogs are

psychic; cats too. You must meet Vanessa's Shadow.''

Moxie barked.

"He hates Shadow," Matt explained, "but has never attacked him. It wouldn't be polite. . . . Do you remember when Miss Hattie was in the hospital?"

"Yes, appendix. My mother was fit to be tied when the letter came — Aunt Hattie was about ready to come home by that time — but Mother would have flown here to be with her if she'd known."

"Your grandaunt was never one to make a fuss. Did you know she could have been my stepmother?"

"Well, gosh . . . no," Maggie said, startled.

"Family history. My mother died about the time yours left Little Oxford. She and Miss Hattie were close friends and your mother was always trying to matchmake for your grandaunt, much to her disgust. My father was fond of Miss Hattie, as a person and a client. Some years ago he thought she might like to marry him, for companionship of course, but also something more than that, I think. She was a very magnetic woman — but, according to him, she just thanked him, and said, 'I'm too set in my ways and besides I'm older than you.' "

"How much?"

"A year, maybe two. . . . Hey, do look in the cupboards."

She did so, found the dog biscuits and took the milk from the refrigerator. "Unless you'd rather have coffee?"

"Nope."

"Cookies," said Maggie and produced them. "Store-bought. Next time, let me know you're coming and I'll cut you a few."

"You can cook?"

"Certainly. American, French, Polynesian, Italian — you name it — oh, a dash of German. Vi — my friend in Los Angeles — her mother is German."

"How about Greek?"

"No."

"I'll take you to a great Greek restaurant not far from here some evening and you can charm the recipes from the owners. These cookies aren't bad," he added, relaxing at the kitchen table.

"Now, do you know anything about probate?"

"Yes. My mother's estate was small, of course, insurance for me, jewelry divided between me and my stepsister Lani, and personal things which went to Greg, if he wanted them. It didn't take long."

"We'll see. This time, longer of course, as there's a great deal more. Dad's the one to straighten things out for you. Meantime, we'll see that you're fed."

"And clothed, please. Vi is sending my clothes on — that is, if she remembers — but at present I feel like the little match girl."

"Okay. Fed and clothed. . . . Moxie, we must move on. I have to report to Mrs. Hunt before I go out to dinner. . . . No, you can't go. Place doesn't allow anyone with four legs."

"Who's Mrs. Hunt?"

"Housekeeper."

"That reminds me. I expect to hear from a Mrs. Green . . . did I ask you if I can afford her?"

"No to both questions, but Dad will cope. You'll like her, she's the village reporter but only that which is fit for conservative ears. I can't say 'fit to print' anymore."

He removed himself from the kitchen chair, and Moxie rose too. Maggie went with them to the door. It was dark now and she commented, "It's so dark. I put lights on before five."

"Gets that way now. Put the porch light on. You scared to stay alone?"

"I don't think so."

He removed a slip of paper from his wallet and stood under the door light to write down a number. "This is the phone," he said, "at home. Call if you need anyone. Dad will come, I'll come, or whoever's at home — even Mrs. Hunt who fears not man nor beast — and of course Moxie will respond."

He waved and went off with Moxie beside him. Maggie shivered and went indoors to light more lamps and adjust the thermostat. She'd probably never get used to this climate. She was not a complete stranger to chilly nights. She'd spent a lot of time at a ranch in the mountains, and in other high places where the nights were cool. But this was a steady, damp, penetrating cold and she thought: Good grief, it's only November!

She went upstairs, changed into slacks and a pullover, came down and sat in the living room, her feet on a hassock, and read the Little Oxford *Beacon,* which she had bought before going to Matt's office. It was a weekly. Perhaps next week, she'd see her own name in the paper. Mr. Comstock had saved the obituary for her from the *Beacon* and from the Deeport paper as well. Everyone thought a lot of Aunt Hattie; how could she ever live up to her.

She'd look at the six o'clock news, she decided, but first assemble the ingredients for supper. She was hungry again. I'd better eat early here, she thought.

When the telephone rang, she answered it in the hall and Matt Comstock said, ''I forgot to tell you about Moxie and Miss Hattie's appendix. I got sidetracked. Anyway, I went to see her in the hospital; Moxie waited in the car — the only hospital I've heard of which allows four-pawed visitors is in England and very special. So, he would cry a little while waiting; not enough to send the authorities screaming from the hospital but sufficient to convince passersby that he had an incarcerated friend and couldn't send get-well cards. Miss Hattie's hospital windows looked over the parking lot and when she was able to sit up, she could see Moxie cavorting, which he rarely does, or just waving. We brought Miss Hattie home, although my father, both Irvingtons, and a few others fought for the privilege but, as Moxie was on my side, I won. Thought you'd like to hear. . . . You okay?"

"I'm fine, Matt, thank you."

"Good night then, " he said. "Don't forget to lock up. Be seeing you."

The next evening, Maggie went to the Palmers'. Jeremy picked her up and she was enchanted with their house.

"Dreamy," agreed Katie. "We planned every inch. Of course here and there we goofed, but it will do."

Dinner was superb as Katie had promised and there was a pretty girl to help in the kitchen. "Can't afford her, but she sort of goes with the house when we have guests," Katie explained. Maggie also met the Palmers' young son and had a short starched conversation with Nanny.

"Terrifies me," Katie said. "I always want to curtsy and say, 'Yes M'm.' "

Andrew Comstock returned to the office and Maggie spent some hours with him. She said, "There's quite a lot of mail. I brought it, as you said."

"Mostly from friends not in the area who haven't heard. It would be kind if you'd answer those, Maggie. Bills will be few: milkman, utilities. Your aunt paid cash for almost everything, including the newspapers. I stopped delivery. Her post-office-box rental had been paid and the taxes — income, property, water and the like. Creditors have a certain amount of time — but there aren't many and her legacy to you is tax free. . . . Matt tells me you may need money."

"Well, shortly. I'll need some clothes, of course, those my friend is sending me won't do; they're for another climate, except for some slacks and a couple of warm suits. And I would like to have someone to clean."

"Mrs. Green," he said promptly. "Suppose I make arrangements with her?"

"I don't know what to do about Aunt Hattie's clothes, Mr. Comstock."

"Mrs. Daniels will help. Those that aren't in good shape — although I can't imagine that — or anything broken or not very usable that you find in the attic can go to one of the charity organizations that repair items like that. Most of Hattie's things would, I think, go to the Village Thrift Shop, which is managed by the hospital with volunteer help. There's a clause in the will — remember? — which says anything you do not want can be sold or given to charity, and she left a small bequest to the hospital."

Maggie shook her head. "I was sort of dazed," she admitted. "Everything happened so quickly."

"You don't remember she left something to Matt?"

"No."

"It's a watercolor, painted, I think, by her mother when Little Oxford was really a village. He always liked it. She also left him a small sum of money 'for treats,' as she expressed it, 'for Moxie.' "

Maggie said, "That's so like her. Is there anything of Aunt Hattie's that you'd like?" she asked.

"Yes. The footstool by the big chair. She embroidered it and when I went to see her, that was my chair and, of course, my footstool."

There were papers to sign. The wheels began to turn. Mrs. Green, a sparse pleasant woman, made her first appearance, and the present owners of the antique shop, a middle-aged couple, telephoned both Andrew Comstock and Maggie with offers. She told Andrew there was very little she wished to sell. "I can't bear to dispose of anything in her bedroom except, of course, the clothes — any more than I can bear to use it. There are a few things in the small bedroom which I won't need when I make it into a study and the living room could look less cluttered — mainly the whatnots and Victorian pieces. But, of course, that's all up to you, Mr. Comstock. ... Oh, I forgot — Jeremy

Palmer wants some books. They're old and in good condition, and I certainly don't want them. But that's up to you too. I can't even read them — all those funny esses."

Letty came over often. Maggie went to the Lee Osbornes' big house and found she did like Stacy whom she'd thought rather remote, but who turned out to be shy. She was a gifted artist and Maggie said, "When I come into my legacy, I'm going to buy something. You'll take me to the gallery?"

"Of course she will," said Lee. "See how her ears prick up."

"I'm going to sort of modernize my room — not the furniture, I love it — but accessories, colors, pictures, when the time comes, " Maggie told them. "I can't live entirely in Aunt Hattie's world."

Stacy said, "Her world will adapt to the contemporary. You'll see; I'll help you. I've been doing quite a few houses lately."

"For a fee," said her husband. "It works out very well for me. I design the houses, she decorates."

"That's right, you did the Palmer house, didn't you? I like it so much."

And Lee said, "Well, thanks."

"Where does everyone buy clothes?" Maggie inquired, then laughed. "There I go grasshoppering."

"Depends," answered Stacy. "Kate and I go to what's known as Today's Casuals, and to a little shop called Jane's for dress-up things; Letty Irvington goes to Bonnie May's Boutique."

"I don't believe it."

"It's true. Rosie Niles buys most of her things in the city."

"I came with what's on my back. My friend in California shipped what I had there by air. It came recently — great stuff for spring. What I have in Hawaii won't do for anything except extra bathing suits. I brought some jewelry — and Aunt Hattie's left me most of hers — but other than that, it's shop for my life from head to toe."

"I'll help," Stacy said again.

"She honestly doesn't get a percentage," Lee assured Maggie and looked lovingly at his wife. "She's just a born do-gooder by nature. So take advantage of her — as I do."

4

By Thanksgiving, Maggie began to feel she was a member of the community. Her stepfather and her stepsister wrote the gloomy prediction that she'd hate Little Oxford and return eventually to Hawaii. Why was she so stubborn? Why not sell the house and come home? She could work, there were positions available; she could live at home. They missed her, everyone missed her from the assistant manager and his family to the people in the offices and fields and factory, also their families, the schoolteacher, the doctor.

She cried a little over the airborne pleas, but stood her cold and unfamiliar ground and replied truthfully, "I like it here. I'm crazy about the people, and this house and the village. I'll survive the winter. I've bought winter clothes. Mr. Comstock is speeding up all the legalities; he's wonderful and everyone's been so kind.''

In writing to Lani, she also said, ''He has an attractive son, single too. He isn't good-looking, but he has charm. Not my type, however. And I think he wants to be a politician. Do try and fly over, Lani, and stay with me. You'd be absolutely one hundred and fifty percent perfect for a politician — of course, you might try for a diplomat. Anyway, you'd love it here. After all you were in college on the mainland and know something about winters, even if they weren't as severe as New England's.''

She was asked for Thanksgiving by the Irvingtons, by the Palmers and the Osbornes, but she had already accepted her first invitation which was Andrew Comstock's. He'd said, ''This year a few people will be coming in for drinks before dinner — Matt suggested mulled wine, but I talked him out of it — then there'll just be us. We'd expected the Bankses, but they have to be out of town.'' He was talking to Maggie in his office, and Matt strolled in as his father added, ''Their daughter-in-law is ill, I think, in Jamaica."

"She's Jamaican. They live in Maryland," Matt told him. "Better come, Maggie; it will be dull without you."

"Thanks," said his father.

On Thanksgiving day, Maggie walked to the Comstocks'. She wore one of her new wool frocks, long-sleeved and high-necked — she hadn't been able to find many as covered up — this one dark aquamarine. She had reflected dismally and aloud to Stacy, who was with her when she bought it, "I can't wear many colors."

"Think of shades," said Stacy, "all greens, blues, and in between, and there's one pink, but it's hard to find. There's also an offbeat apricot — for sober moments. Any brown, any gray. You'll make out."

Despite the wool dress and the sturdy tweed coat, Maggie shivered. I hope I'm not forced into long underwear and wool socks, she thought.

Matt opened the door, with Moxie beside him, and they both regarded her benevolently. "Bright-eyed and bushy-tailed," said Matt. "Your nose is a mite red. Come in. Happy Thanksgiving. Why didn't you let me come get you?''

"Figured I'd have to brave the elements sooner or later," Maggie told him, "and it's starting to feel like sooner."

"Fling your new coat aside. . . . That's a very becoming dress," Matt said, and took her into the living room where people had congregated and Mrs. Hunt and an assistant were passing various canapés. The fireplace was inhabited by a large fire, and pumpkins sat on the hearth, while at intervals, on tables, there were orange-red berries.

Maggie pointed and asked, "What?"

"Bittersweet. And it's rude to point."

"Well, I'd never seen it. You have corn at the door, I've seen that — here, of course. I'll have to buy some."

Andrew Comstock was busy behind an improvised bar, and Matt said, "My progenitor has provided everything — soft, hard, middling. What's your pleasure?"

"Middling, somewhat diluted."

With the tall glass in her hand, he steered her around. "I think you know most everyone," he said, "especially Mrs.

Daniels. . . . Here's her husband, Ned."

There were others from the office, a brace of secretaries, also the young man who ran errands, and then Matt said, "And Dr. and Mrs. Carstairs. They are almost as new here as you, Maggie, but not quite."

Maggie spoke, gave her hand, and smiled. Then her eyes widened. Dr. Carstairs was probably the handsomest man she'd ever met — improbable actually. He looked about thirty-five; his wife a decade his senior. She was a rather short dumpy woman, with blunt features, and nondescript coloring, redeemed by a warm smile and magnificent eyes.

Matt said, "They've bought the old Melvin house — he was a doctor about the time Bing Irvington began practice here. . . . I keep forgetting you're not Little Oxford, Maggie."

"I'm beginning to be," Maggie said with vigor.

And Matt said, "Maggie's from Hawaii," with the air of someone exhibiting a rare tropical bird.

After a few minutes Maggie found

herself on a love seat beside Mrs. Carstairs who had been to the Islands — first on her wedding trip, twice since. She thought that they had changed greatly since the first time — twelve years ago — but that, despite change, the charm was still there.

Twelve *years,* thought Maggie.

"So you're a newcomer too?" said Lily Carstairs. "We've been here almost a year."

Maggie explained her presence and Lily asked, "What do you do?"

Everyone nowadays has to do something. Those who don't or who reply with the "I'm just a housewife" bit have become almost extinct.

Maggie told her.

"Perhaps you'll see my husband occasionally. He goes to the hospital. He's an allergist."

"Don't forget dermatology," said her husband, who had been talking to Mrs. Daniels nearby.

"Well," said Maggie, "if I can get a job. . . . Dr. Irvington is trying. There could be an opening in the respiratory

66

department, he told me a couple of days ago."

"Bing or Ben?" asked Alan Carstairs.

"Both."

"I hope they succeed," he said.

And his wife said, smiling, "Both the Irvington men strike me as forceful, so I'm sure they will. . . . I'm afraid it's time for us to leave, Alan."

The others soon drifted away and presently dinner was served.

After Andrew said grace Matt asked Maggie, "What did you think of the Carstairs?"

"Nice and he's the best-looking man I ever saw," she told him.

"Everyone else thinks so too, even males," said Andrew.

Then Maggie asked, "Isn't he a lot younger than his wife?"

Matt replied promptly, "Of course, also I've heard him called 'Centerfold Carstairs.' " Whereupon Mrs. Hunt, passing the cranberry sauce, remarked, as tartly as the berries, "It isn't his fault how he looks. I'm just sorry for her, is all."

During the pleasant interval over after-dinner coffee, Matt remarked, "I've often thought it odd that you don't smoke, Maggie."

"You wouldn't think so if you knew Greg, my stepfather. I hate calling him that."

"Then why do you?"

"Oh, I dunno. I got used to it because our surnames were different before he adopted me legally and sometimes I had to explain. I wish he were here right now."

"Homesick?" asked Andrew.

"Well, yes, a little, I guess."

After a while she looked away from the fire to her hosts. "I'm sorry," she said. "I promised to be at Amy's around eight — they're having some people in — "

"I have a date too," announced Matt, "and I can take Moxie. This is a new girl. She likes dogs and I'm to go to her house for coffee, brandy and elegant stereo music. Moxie's invited."

"Go along, both of you," Andrew said. "I'll read, watch TV — maybe I'll call Vanessa and see what she's doing."

"She'll be at Stacy's."

"Perhaps not, Matt. Run along, you two."

The farewells were said and Matt, Maggie and Moxie went outside "The three M's," said Matt, "not to be confused with various trademarks. . . . Hey, it's snowing."

So it was, very lightly. Maggie felt the flakes touch briefly her hair and cheeks and announced in astonishment, "It's cold and wet!"

"What did you think it would be, you ignorant woman?" Matt asked.

She answered, "I don't know — like cotton wool perhaps."

"Always keep a hood or something handy this time of year," he cautioned her, "otherwise the fire in your hair will go out."

"It doesn't in the rain," she said laughing.

"Your kind of rain, okay . . . liquid sunshine; maybe even California's. But wait until you experience autumn rains here."

"I have."

"Then spring. . . . What are we fighting about?"

"I didn't know we were!"

They'd reached her house and Matt said, "Moxie and I will come in while you freshen up, or whatever euphemism you employ, and then see you off."

"But it's snowing," Maggie complained as they went inside.

"Are you saying you won't drive?"

"Also, it's night."

"My dear idiot, this is a snow shower — it will probably stop in a few minutes. It hasn't stuck on road, street, bush or tree. It's just a small warning of days to come. What will happen to you when it really snows? Maybe Miss Hattie's estate can provide a horse and sleigh, or you can walk. I yearn to see you slogging through the drifts."

"Drifts?"

"It gets windy. . . . Come on, fix your face and so on and I'll drop you off at Ben's. Someone will be pressed into service to take you home or you can spend half your legacy on a taxi."

On the way, Matt said, "I'll leave Moxie in the car. Not that he and Oscar don't like each other, they do, and Oscar's more often at Bing's than Ben's, though he is beginning to feel responsible for Benjy. But I'll be at the house so short a time it won't be worthwhile. Moxie's usually the center of attention, which holds me up. He knows it. Egotistical creature."

Maggie put her hand on Moxie's head and thought that in the light of the dashboard she could see him smile.

Amy opened the door.

"Where's Moxie?" she inquired.

"In the car. I'll be here only a moment."

"Come on in. Did you enjoy our little display of winter, Maggie? Matt, you refused to come when I asked you; said you had a date."

"I do. I brought Maggie because she's afraid to drive in darkness, complicated by a change in the weather."

"I'm not afraid of the dark," Maggie said indignantly, "or of hills or narrow roads."

"You know everyone," said Amy and cries of greeting arose from the small group. Ben hugged Maggie and Amy asked relentlessly, "What girl, Matt? Evie, Crystal or Barby?"

"None of those lovely ladies."

"Got a new one?" asked Ben. "Can't be Maggie or you would have accepted when we asked. Do you realize I'm *home?* We had dinner at Pop's so one of us could rush out chewing a turkey leg, whichever one was called. He was. I ate and then came home with my wife. Meantime I wait for the phone to ring. . . . Who wants something to drink — coffee, cider or something stronger?"

Amy said, "You haven't told us about the girl."

"Agatha Redmond."

"Never heard of her."

"Of course not, you're so exclusive. She's from Deeport and that's where I'm headed."

"South of the border," said Jeremy Palmer.

Maggie looked about the room, smiling — all the people she knew and liked best except Ben's parents.

"I'm sorry a couple of Irvingtons are missing," she said.

"We left Benjy with his grandparents overnight, just in case this small select party becomes a brawl. . . . What does your Agatha do?'' Amy asked Matt.

"You are very much like Maggie, which is to say scatterbrained, also nosy. . . . She's on the staff of the *Deeport Weekly.* That's one paper I can make, I think. As Maggie refuses to drive in this raging blizzard, will someone take her home or bed her down here in a sleeping bag?''

"I shall if I'm here,'' Ben said and Amy said, "I'm free.'' Both Palmers offered and Lee Osborne said, "I would, but we have to move on soon; we promised to look in on Vanessa. She had dinner with us and I told her we'd stop by tonight.''

"She can't be turning timid,'' Ben said. "She isn't afraid of anything under heaven.''

"She's just getting old,'' Stacy said, "and frail. Haven't you seen her lately?''

"No, and I don't think Pop has. She's supposed to have a physical. Wish you'd remind her.''

"I suppose I could take my life in my hands,'' Lee Osborne said thoughtfully.

"I've been hoping you'd take me to see her,'' Maggie told Stacy.

"I shall, when she's in the mood. . . . Did I ask you if you like cats?"

"Of course I do."

"There's no of course about it," said Matt. "I am merely respectful. . . . Well, I've got to get on my horse if I'm to be at Deeport before morning in this terrible storm. Good night, all. Be seeing you."

It was a good evening. They ate, saying, "But I really can't." They had music on the stereo; they danced and toward twelve Maggie yawned. "Sorry about that," she said apologetically.

"It's time we all went home," Katie said. "Ben will be hard at work tomorrow remedying the ailments of those who ate and drank too much, Jeremy will be working, I'll cope with Nanny. . . . It was great fun, Amy."

Jeremy and Katie drove Maggie home. It was not snowing. The night was clear and dark, the stars brilliant, and the wind had died down. It was also very cold.

"You'll get used to it," Jeremy comforted, as he went to the door with Maggie. "Your blood will thicken."

"Sounds dreadful," Maggie said. "Good night, Jeremy — and thank you."

She yawned her way upstairs. It was shortly past midnight, and she was almost ready for bed when the telephone rang. She stumbled into her aunt's room, leaving her own bedroom door open for light. "Must have an extension by my bed," she muttered.

"Hello," she said.

"Aloha," said her stepfather. "Happy Thanksgiving, I hope."

"Greg! Have you any idea what time it is?"

"Naturally. We were about to sit down to dinner, a dozen of us, including Lani. Everyone wants to speak to you except me. I'm very annoyed with you . . . you should be home. What's the weather like?"

"It snowed today, a little. I won't ask you about yours," she said sadly. "Oh, Lani, hi."

Lani said she'd had Maggie's letter and would probably see her in the spring, "if your neighbor and lawyer is still single." She added, "Maggie, we miss you dreadfully."

After that, everyone spoke with her, and at the end Greg and his daughter spoke with her once more.

Maggie went back to bed close to tears, listened to the wind which had risen again, curled up under her electric blanket, and slept.

5

The sun shone on Friday and there remained no trace of the snow shower. The temperature had moderated and Maggie woke, showered, wished she could sing, dressed, and had breakfast. There were things she could do in the house, but Mrs. Green came Tuesdays, so there was nothing immediate . . . except for a small load of laundry in the cellar. At the kitchen table, looking at the cheerful geraniums, she thought of the day before — reliving it, from the time she'd walked to the Comstocks' to the time she reached home last night and talked to her family and friends.

She had, of course, fallen slightly in love with Alan Carstairs, a perfectly natural reaction for her. She'd always been influenced by appearances, to her stepfather's concern. Also to his concern, she preferred older men. "Someday," he had predicted when Maggie was sixteen, "you'll fall in love with an actor three times your age."

"Oh I have, often, but I never get to meet any of them," she admitted. "Besides they're all married; married often, some of them."

"Thank heaven," her pretty mother had commented, "she draws the line at married men, but still she worries me. Someday she'll produce someone with a long white beard and honorable intentions."

"Santa Claus?"

"Of course not, Greg darling; he's married," said his wife.

"Where do you suppose the elves came from?" Maggie had inquired.

"It's the father image," Rachel told her husband.

"That's becoming a cliché," Greg Knox informed her.

Now Maggie thought she'd have to settle for Dr. Carstairs as just a pinup in her mind. He was married and besides, she reflected, he wouldn't look at me more than once.

Katie, with whom Maggie had lunch the following day, agreed that Carstairs was gorgeous, "but I don't really admire handsome men," she added. "I'm glad Jeremy's no super-startler. It's safer. I like the Carstairs; we sold them the house. She's a darling."

"She seemed very pleasant," Maggie agreed, thoughtfully munching celery, "but she's quite plain."

"Gorgeous guys almost always marry plain women," Katie assured her. "Then there's no competition, so no one fights for the mirror."

"And she's lots older."

"He was a struggling resident and she financed him then and thereafter. She told me they were married when he was twenty-three. She makes no bones about her seniority. They had a lot in common as he had lost his parents; she had, also. He'd been brought up by cousins — in Pennsylvania, I think; she in Baltimore, by an old uncle and his eccentric sister. But she came into her inheritance by degrees — an income at eighteen, a good deal more at twenty-one and the lot at thirty."

"She actually told you this?"

"Well, also by degrees. I didn't ask — any information from her was volunteered — and some came from other sources. In this town," said Katie, "a newcomer comes under close scrutiny — like a politician — sometimes."

"I still don't understand the marriage. Of course, I can see why she'd fall in love with him, but — except for the money — I can't imagine why he — "

"Don't try to, Maggie. He's crazy about her. All the single gals, and some of the married ones, have tried their best — or worst — since the Carstairs came to Little Oxford. Amy says half the female population had developed allergies since their arrival. I dunno how well he did in Baltimore — he was a Hopkins man — but he's doing just fine here. She told me they came to New England because his ancestral roots are here and also their son would like it, skiing nearby and all that."

"You mean to say they have a child?"

"Why not?" Katie inquired. "It would hardly be a Sarah and Abraham situation. Let's see. She's ten or more years his senior — I don't know how long they've been married, but the boy's ten, I think."

"She told me — twelve years."

"So she was anything from thirty-three to thirty-five when Kim was born. He's named for her family; her maiden name was Kimberly. She told me neither she nor her husband wanted a junior. She said, 'Alan thinks Kim should be on his own.' I don't know exactly what she meant, seeing that I have a Junior Jeremy."

"I think I do," Maggie said.

Katie looked at her watch. "Must run," she said, "Mrs. Warner will be tearing out her hair. I was due at the office ten minutes ago. See you, Maggie." She cast a bill on the table and departed.

Maggie ordered mince pie and coffee and pursued her own thoughts, solitary at the table until Matt Comstock came barreling in, saw her, and asked, "Coming or going?"

"If you want this table," she said severely, "I'll be going presently.

Meantime, I won't hurry; it's bad for the digestion.''

"Drive downtown?''

"Certainly not. I walked. I save gas.''

"I hope it's a mild winter,'' he told her and gave the hovering waitress his order. "Hamburger — and tell Howie just to breathe on both sides — salad and coffee, please, Annie.''

"You'll get trichinosis or something,'' Maggie warned.

"Haven't so far. Of course with the high cost of self-indulgence, I'll soon be feeding Moxie better than myself.''

"Where is he? Isn't he allowed in here?''

"Certainly he's allowed; now and then he sneaks a snack. But he's at the vet's.''

"What's wrong?''

"Nothing. Just a checkup. He likes everyone at the vet's; there's no problem. How *can* you eat mince pie?''

"With a fork, usually.''

"Don't be smart. You are, I've observed, a good trencherman. I'll remember that when I take you to dinner. We'll go where the food is filling but not costly. I assume you like pasta?''

"Love it."

"Why aren't you obese?"

"Metabolism. Suppose you and your father come have dinner with me one night soon. Just tell me what you like — I mean what type of cooking. I don't go in for Beluga caviar, and I can't cook Russian, but I do have some vodka. Anyway, I'm taking up entertaining, budget or no budget, as I'm not working — unfortunately."

"I'll consult Dad as to dates. We can probably give you a choice," he said graciously. "Then after we've had dinner, if it's very good, perhaps I could get you a job."

"Such as?"

"There are still people who can afford cooks — not many, but a few — and more who can use a caterer now and then. We aren't in the market."

"Not with Mrs. Hunt," she agreed.

"She's not help; she's family," said Matt. "Incidentally, she approves of you though she doesn't often like my girls."

"How was the date with Agatha last night?"

"Oh, Agatha. All right, but I think she's inclined toward the usual feminine dishonest wiles."

"What kind?"

"She doesn't really like dogs. She made a great ado over Moxie, but he retired under a chair and went to sleep. He can scent hypocrisy."

Andrew Comstock and his son came to dinner the following week. Andrew had said, "Anything except fried," but, urged by Maggie, had admitted he'd relish a New England boiled dinner, as Mrs. Hunt hadn't concocted one lately.

In his old friend's house, Andrew wandered about the living room after dinner while Maggie cleared the table with Matt's garrulous and complaining assistance. "Didn't you ask me once why I haven't married?" he said. "Well, now you know. . . . Moxie, get out of the way."

"Where's the coffee?" his father called.

"En route," Matt replied. "I'm carrying the tray as it weighs more than Maggie."

Andrew went back to his big chair for which Maggie had provided another footstool. "Black, please," he told her and, when she'd put the cup on the table beside him, added, "Seems strange to be in this house without Hattie."

"It must be," Maggie agreed. "Of course, I don't have that feeling of missing her here because I was never in the house while she was alive. But I sometimes think maybe she comes occasionally — perhaps with my mother. It's a very agreeable thought actually."

Moxie was settled by Matt. "Your coffee," said Andrew, "is perfection; even better than Hattie's. She was a good cook," he added, "but not, I think, as good as you are."

"You've only had one sample," Maggie told him.

The telephone rang. She went to answer it in the hall and returned with flags flying. "I'm to see Mr. Davis at the hospital Monday. Ben says there's an opening."

"Heck!" said Matt. "I was counting on numerous fantastic meals and contemplating a choice of menus as I'm sure you can soar beyond the boiled dinner, but now you'll neither have time nor energy. You'll come home, pop a TV dinner in the oven, and put your feet up.''

"Never. And I'll have weekends.''

"No way. Then, you'll be yakking with the girls, shopping for frozen vittles and cosmetics.''

"I use practically none.''

"I know. I'm an expert. But after you've been working a while you'll grow scrawny, haggard and also bad-tempered.''

"Matt, said his father, "kindly shut up. . . . I'm delighted for you, Maggie. Bert Davis is an exceptional administrator.''

"Dad's on the Board. I bet he twisted Bert's arm.''

"I spoke to him,'' replied his father, "and that's all. . . . You'll like him, Maggie; he's a fine man.''

"Well, congratulations, Maggie,'' Matt said gloomily, "even if I did anticipate the occasional gourmet meal.''

"I leave you two to bicker,'' Andrew said. "You sound married.'' He went into the kitchen and they heard doors open and close.

"He's right,'' Matt said. "The bickering

is for the wedded, the glorious knockdown fights reserved for the single."

"Not exclusively," Maggie said.

"Don't argue. What do you suppose he's up to?"

"He's bringing us the makings of a toast."

Andrew came in smiling, with a bottle in one hand and three cordial glasses in the other. "I can't find the coasters," he announced.

Maggie went to get them and Andrew said, "Well, don't just stand there, Matt. Take the bottle and set it down. Also the glasses."

Returning, Maggie said, "You remembered the lower left-hand cupboard!"

"I did. That's where Hattie kept her potables. She always consulted me when she was to have guests. As you both may recall she was very moderate — an occasional glass of sherry or wine. But this is brandy. I gave it to her last Christmas and, as you see, it's still almost full. I'm sure she'd want Matt and me to drink to your good health and fortune, Maggie, and it won't break the spell if you join us."

A little later, Maggie said, "I don't like brandy, cognac or what have you, but when I think of months ahead — perhaps I could use a St. Bernard."

"Hey, that reminds me. Has your car been winterized, Maggie?" Matt asked.

"I had Joe do that before Maggie came," said his father, "except for snow tires. Hattie bought them last year and used the car very little, even though it was a mild winter."

"I hope this one will be."

"Don't count on it, Maggie," Matt advised her. "I'll run you up to Joe's, say tomorrow, and we'll get the tires put on. Miss Hattie's used him since he opened the station. He's a great mechanic and a good all-round guy."

"Prefers pleasant customers," his father said.

"Do you skate, Maggie?" Matt asked.

"No, I've never gone to a rink."

"Ski?"

"Of course not."

"Not even water ski?"

"I tried that when I was in California. Vi

loved to — claimed there was nothing like it to display her figure, but it scared me. I swim as well as anyone not in the Olympics, but skiing's different. Vi used to go to the mountains for the snow and skiing; not me."

Matt said, "If we have good snow this winter, I'll take you to Clancy's Joint some weekends and teach you. A lot of Little Oxfordians go there. We can make up parties — "

"Clancy's Joint," explained his father, "is both a winter and summer resort, its proper name being Cloud Eagle Lodge."

"Nauseating," Matt remarked. "Actually we have only the beginning of mountains. Ed Clancy owns the place and his son runs it. It's not far, so people go there just to sit around and talk — great fireplaces, great food, and plenty of girls, who don't ski, in après-ski clothes. You'll love it. Good slopes for beginners; you'll catch on fast."

"Not a chance," Maggie said firmly.

"But there's nothing to it," said Matt.

"Except broken bones," said his father, "and, at the best, pratfalls."

"Sitzmarks, please."

"Maggie. don't listen. He should never have studied law. He doesn't even understand gravity!"

After they'd gone — Andrew, Matt and Moxie each having kissed her for luck — Maggie cantered happily upstairs. "Keep your fingers crossed," she told herself. She'd disliked being idle. She liked work; it made recreation that much more fun and, if Mr. Davis approved, she'd soon have an eight-hour, five-day-a-week paying job with the usual fringe benefits. And the first thing she'd do would be to commit an extravagance more heartening than brandy. She'd call her family.

Before Monday it had snowed and Matt telephoned to announce that he was sacrificing his lunch hour and coming to take her and the car to Joe's.

"By the way, where have you been getting gas?" he asked.

"Your father had the tank filled, and I've hardly used it."

"Get it at Joe's from now on. Arrange your face into your most seductive smile before you meet him."

It had stopped snowing before dawn, the roads were ploughed, and Maggie said, "I'll never feel *comfortable* comfortable."

"Don't be chicken. Take it easy; watch the other guy; don't slam on your brakes; you'll survive."

When they reached the station: "Treat her right, Joe, friend of the family's. Needs a rush job."

"Miss Hattie's car," said Joe, walking around it, "so you'll be Miss Hattie's niece."

"I'm Maggie," she told him, extending her small brown hand.

Joe, a compact man, grinned and nearly dislocated her wrist. "Pleased to meet you, Maggie," he said.

On the way home, Maggie commented thoughtfully, "It bumps some."

"That's right. Listen while Uncle warns about winter driving. You're fortunate. Unlike most hospitals ours isn't on a hill, though there's a little slope. It will take a while for you to feel safe."

"I'm just not accustomed . . . Well, go on with the lecture."

"Sand," he concluded "can be very

helpful and weight in the trunk of your car never hurt. I also keep a small shovel. AAA says, 'Kitty litter's best.' Your aunt wouldn't have laughed at that!''

"Want to bet? Kitty litter," she said and went into gales of laughter.

"Control yourself," Matt advised, taking her and the car into the garage. "What would Moxie think?"

"He isn't with us."

"I know. He's sulking in his tent, but I'll tell him when I reach home."

He walked her to the house and she thanked him and he said, *"Por nada.* I felt it was incumbent upon me to get you started. After all, I'm the junior partner. And I'll be away a good deal between now and Christmas."

"Doing what?"

"Defending the innocent. Aloha. I'll see you in court."

6

Amy came in her small car to accompany Maggie to the hospital on Monday. She arrived for lunch and said, "You'll take your car," and later asked, "Nervous?"

"Nope," Maggie answered, pouring coffee. "Well, a little, maybe. Mostly I think it's getting there."

Amy munched thoughtfully on her grilled sandwich. She said, "We'll go up together. I'll be in the reception room on the first floor when you get through. If not, ask the gal at the desk — Sally — to page me. Meanwhile I'll be looking in on some of Ben's patients. Incidentally, I do volunteer work there on Thursdays as a rule, so I'll be able to keep an eye on you."

Under Amy's directions, Maggie drove to the hospital — she'd only seen it in passing — and parked, not without difficulty, where Amy told her to.

On the main floor, Amy and the girl on the desk greeted each other. Introductions were in order, and Amy said, "Maggie — Miss Knox — has an appointment with Mr. Davis. Look after her, will you?"

Maggie watched Amy depart, sat down on a small cushioned seat against a wall, and waited.

In a few minutes Sally said, "Miss Knox?" and Maggie bounced to her feet and followed someone who appeared as if by legerdemain.

In the Administrator's office, there was a good-sized anteroom occupied by a busy typist and Mr. Davis's secretary, one Mrs. Cromwell, who was short and round, with a rosy face and brushed back gray hair.

She said, "Will you sit down for a moment, Miss Knox? Mr. Davis has been held up a little." She added, "I knew your greataunt. She was a wonderful person."

Thanks to Aunt Hattie, Maggie thought, everyone's friendly.

After about twenty minutes a voice spoke on the intercom. "Ask Miss Knox to come on in," it said.

Mrs. Cromwell smiled encouragingly,

and took Maggie through the connecting door. Mr. Davis rose from behind his desk. He was very tall and had a curiously ageless appearance. He said, shaking her hand, "I feel as if I knew you; your aunt spoke of you often. All of us who knew her experienced a great loss. I met you at the funeral service, but there were so many there you wouldn't remember."

"Now I do," said Maggie.

After a moment, he said, "Bing and Ben Irvington have spoken of you, also Andrew Comstock. You think you would like to work in the hospital?"

Maggie took her brief résumé from her handbag. "I know I would. I worked in one in Honolulu; later in Los Angeles, in a small private clinic owned by four specialists."

Mr. Davis read the resume, and then the references.

"I had them sent on from Los Angeles," she said, "when I decided to stay here. I didn't bring them or much of anything else with me. I just took a sudden leave of absence from the clinic. But as I had a friend looking for similar work, I asked her to fill in. She's still there."

"We're glad you decided to remain," he told her. "I daresay you couldn't resist the house. . . . I didn't require a medical secretary in this office — we have several in other departments — until about a year and a half ago. So I engaged one, a Miss Roberts, but she is to be married shortly and will move to another state. She left us last week. I thought we could get on without her, but Mrs. Cromwell and I have decided not — paperwork and problems increase daily — and sometimes our staff doctors borrowed Miss Roberts. You'll see," he said, returning the references and résumé.

Summoned by her boss, Mrs. Cromwell took Maggie under her wing, indicating a desk, typewriter and chair now occupied by a typist. "This is Fran Jackson," she told Maggie. "We borrowed her. You'll inherit all this day after tomorrow, plus Miss Robert's meticulous files."

A few minutes later Maggie flew down the corridor and Amy, who was talking to Sally at the desk, turned and said, "I needn't ask how things went."

"Day after tomorrow. I think both Mr. Davis and Mrs. Cromwell are super."

"Cromwell will be a little sticky," Amy warned as they went toward the parking lot. "She's been with him for a long time. You'd be wise to check with her if problems arise."

"Not with the boss?"

"Only if she suggests it. . . . Ever been around a hospital at Christmas?"

"Of course, at home," Maggie answered as they got into the car. "It will be different," she admitted. "Flowers, warmth, leis — no Christmas trees. Come to think of it I never saw one until California. Not a real one."

"You'll see them here," Amy promised. "In the hospital they aren't real either of course. Fire laws. But there'll be parties and cards and homesick people and some who are dying. But I expect you know all that."

That night Maggie telephoned home. Talking to Lani, she said, "I'm going to airmail some things home for Christmas, next week."

Lani said, "You're a wretched girl. We did so want you here."

"Any special reason?"

"He's tall, blond and marvelous," said her stepsister, "but not serious."

"Don't forget to airmail the leis I asked for," Maggie said, "and let me know how much. I'll send you a check from my first salary."

"Estate not settled?"

"No. Besides, more fun when I've earned it."

"Too right," said Lani.

"The tall, blond and marvelous — he's Australian?" queried Maggie.

"How'd you guess?"

"I've known a few," Maggie said.

By Wednesday, Maggie was at work. Matt was away and Moxie came calling. He came as soon as Mrs. Hunt let him out, which was before Maggie got home; and evenings, when Andrew went walking with him or, when solitary, he came alone.

Matt came home before Christmas and took Maggie out to dinner.

"Moxie's been to see me," she said.

"Keeps an eye on you, that's our understanding."

"Amy does too, or so she says. How did the case go?"

"Lost it," he said cheerfully.

"Honestly?"

"If I hadn't been honest, I might not have lost," he told her. "Anyway we'll appeal. . . . With whom are you celebrating Noel?"

"Everyone, I hope. Letty and Dr. Bing are having a buffet from two in the afternoon until eight at night — "

"People will start coming at one and leaving at midnight."

"Of course. Everyone's asked. Aren't you?" she inquired.

"Certainly. What time are you going?"

"Early, to help. Amy will too, and Letty's daughter and her family are hoping to fly home for the first time in years," said Maggie.

"I'll drop by about six," Matt said. "I dunno about Dad. Mrs. Hunt will have something going for us if we get hungry. Did you order a wreath for your door?"

"Why no . . . I didn't think."

"You're a snowbird now. I'll send you one with bells, from Moxie."

Soon the hospital was bright with decorations, wreaths, Santa and trees, all according to the fire laws. Student nurses caroled on the stairs and in corridors and lobby, and the waiting rooms were decked out with holly.

"Too ghastly," Maggie said to Mrs. Cromwell, who looked astonished.

"The patients expect it," she said reproachfully. "So do their families."

Christmas menus for those not on diets or unable to eat and rooms filled with chatter, bright parcels, flower arrangements and tiny trees. Maggie found it most depressing.

There were various parties going on in the nurses' lounge and other places; the hospitality shop was crowded with people and decorations; the gift shop practically selling out. At one gathering to which Mrs. Cromwell and Mr. Davis had taken Maggie, she encountered Dr. Carstairs, his wife — who remembered her; he didn't for a moment — and their ten-year-old son who looked like his mother.

There was mistletoe about and a lot of people kissed a lot of people, drank punch and ate cookies. To Maggie's amazement both Alan Carstairs and his son kissed her, and Lily Carstairs, passing by, said, "Give her one for me too."

Dr. Carstairs seemed even better-looking than Maggie remembered and she noticed how his son stood, as his father stood, and walked as his father did, with his hands behind his back. The boy's resemblance to his father was only in his mannerisms and height — he would be a very tall man — and in the fact that he was dark.

Carstairs said, "I didn't recognize you at first. I'm sorry." He looked at her with approval — the green wool dress, the little Christmas earrings — and asked, "How come you're here — at a staff clambake?"

"I work here now," she told him. "In Mr. Davis's office."

Lily, coming up, said, "We have to go, Alan. Miss Knox is a medical secretary — don't you remember? — she told us when we met at the Comstocks'. . . . Tear yourself away from the punch bowl, Kim,'' she admonished her offspring.

Alan smiled at Maggie, ''I'll see you around, I hope. I might even have a moonlight job for you.''

Lily explained, ''He's doing some writing for medical journals. He doesn't type very well; I'm worse, and the average secretary would be completely confused by the various terms. Suppose I call you, Miss Knox?''

''Maggie, please . . . and please do.''

She thought, after she was home, that if she were asked, she'd find an excuse not to accept. It would be pure stupidity to be around a man like that. But I don't have to be, she told herself triumphantly. It gives me an idea, however. I'll buy a secondhand typewriter, use it here for my own letters and if I do get extra work, it will pay for itself.

Christmas at Letty and Bing's was great fun. As Maggie had predicted, everyone came — for a moment or for hours. Vanessa Steele came, a tall woman with tossed white hair, a gypsy-brown face and remarkable eyes. Stacy went off after presenting Maggie to her and they had a brief but curious conversation.

"Like it here?"

"Yes, very much."

"I knew your grandaunt slightly. She didn't approve of me and I thought she was too good to be true."

Maggie bristled. "She was true all right, Mrs. Steele."

"I've never been much of a judge of women," said Vanessa and emitted a brief cackle. "Do you like cats?"

"Of course."

"Not of course. Many people don't. You harbor a dog?"

"No," Maggie told her and warmed suddenly to this strange old character. "You do ask a lot of questions, don't you?"

"How else can I find anything out? You're a friend of Stacy's, that's enough for me. I hear you've been going around with Matthew Comstock."

"I wouldn't exactly call it that." Maggie laughed. "Silly phrase, sounds dizzy."

"Often is."

"I daresay. Yes, I see him. His father's

my lawyer and neighbor."

"Matt's attractive," said Vanessa. "I still know an attractive man when I see one, and I'm still capable of distinguishing a stimulant from a tranquilizer."

"Attractive? Matt?"

"You don't think so?"

"Well, yes!" Maggie agreed. "I've never really thought much about it."

"Start thinking. It will be interesting to discover what, in fact, attracts you. I like Matthew, in spite of that enormous animal he pampers."

"Moxie is a standard-size shepherd," Maggie told her, "and very well behaved."

"I know that he's not as obnoxious as most of them. 'Bye. Come see me sometime," and she stalked off.

"Well, what do you think of Van?" Stacy asked, returning.

"What's anyone to think? She's wild."

"We love her. Her son and his family are in the Caribbean this Christmas. They asked her to go along, but she wouldn't so she and her Shadow will have a quiet dinner with us and Lee's sister and her husband from Texas."

"Her shadow? I thought maybe she didn't cast one," Maggie said.

"Shadow, her cat," said Stacy.

Vanessa left shortly thereafter with the Osbornes and Ben came by to inquire, "How's it going?"

"At the hospital? Fine, and I'm lucky I had today off."

"Very likely you'll see Bert Davis and his wife here . . . he promised Letty. . . . There's Matt and his senior partner."

"It must be six o'clock," Maggie decided. "I'd no idea . . . "

"Go fill the wassail cup and eat," said Ben. "You have to keep up your strength."

Matt strolled up with a sprig of mistletoe in his hand. He held it over Maggie's red hair and kissed her, waved a negligent hand and warned, "Don't let it go to your head. I'm determined to oblige every female in the room. Where's Pearl," he demanded, "and isn't that Mrs. Green?"

Maggie was talking to Jim Hutchinson, the young clergyman who had followed Gordon Banks, when Matt resurfaced. He said, looking at his watch, "If you are ready to go home by quarter to eight, I'll take you and my parent."

"I drove here," she said.

"Good for you. Better go early, tomorrow's a working day. Even I'll be at the office," said Matt.

Just as Maggie was leaving the Carstairs came in, the doctor wearing a bright red sport coat and his wife a red wool dress. Kim was with them and Maggie said, "You look very sharp, Kim."

"Neat," he agreed. "Gosh, what I got for Christmas — neat — sled, toboggan, new skates, great skis — "

"Top of Santa's list?" Maggie suggested.

Kim unleashed a funny little crow of laughter. "Well," he said tolerantly, "Santa's just a myth, like the stork — but I sort of like myths."

His father said, "I'm glad of that. Sometimes it's unfortunate that the myths must go, or don't you agree with me, Miss Knox?"

He had come to stand beside Kim, his arm around the boy's shoulders and

Maggie said, "I certainly do. I firmly believe in glass slippers and pumpkin coaches — "

"Sleeping beauties, frog princes?" asked Lily Carstairs. "But I suppose being realistic has become a part of today. Still it's a pity we can't keep our illusions even after we know what they are." She looked at her husband, smiled, and back at Maggie. "Would you have any free time," she asked, "directly after the New Year?"

"I'll make it," Maggie promised and ignored the small silent warning within herself.

7

The New Year frolicked in, heedless of anything it might bring, and with attendant spurious resolutions and valid hangovers; also terrible weather beginning with an ice storm on the Eve.

Maggie, setting her small but stubborn jaw, dressed for the Arctic and toiled up to the Comstocks'. Matt had offered to fetch her, "on our dangerous way here from across the line," he'd said.

"What line?" she asked.

"State," he replied. "I have to escort a young woman."

Maggie, no weather prophet, said, "I'll walk."

She fell flat several times, once on her face, mercifully not disfigured, and twice on her bottom — which would, she concluded, be black and blue. When she finally reached the Comstock door, she was wet, cold and miserable. "It's these damned clothes," she told her sympathetic host. "They're so heavy that I fall down and then can't get up. The boots alone weigh a ton."

After she thawed out, it was pleasant to be with people she knew and some she didn't — Matt's new girl, for instance. Her name was Victoria Wilson. She refused to be called Viki, so was known as Willy. She was tall — in her platform shoes a shade taller than Matt — she was blonde and cunningly shaped by nature and her elegant clothing.

"This one I'm serious about," Matt told Maggie.

"That's his game plan," Willy said. "I don't even listen."

"She has only one flaw," Matt said. "She's on a diet. But remember, a long time ago, you told me nobody's perfect, Maggie. Like a ghoul Willy nibbles occasionally on one grain of rice. I took her recently to a very special restaurant. Everyone cried — the waiter, the owner, myself — all that culinary talent wasted. I didn't see the chef; he was in a state of shock."

"Sorry about that," Willy said, "but no one cared whether I ate or not and it saved you a lot of money."

"You I admire, Magpie — you eat hearty."

"Don't call me that."

This was a recent development. "Why not?" he asked. "You chatter."

"Magpies also steal," said Maggie.

Willy said, "I don't dare gain an ounce. What model does? . . . You two having a fight?"

During the following week, Matt came calling with Moxie, who knocked on Maggie's door with his tail. Moxie often came unaccompanied but, a gentleman, always knocked.

"Come in, guys," she said.

"I've been reading a brief," Matt told her gloomily. "What a misnomer. Brew us something hot and lace it with arsenic. I'm extremely depressed."

"Make yourselves at home as usual. I'll stir up something. Anyway it's time for my coffee break and Amy sent me doughnuts. . . . What's wrong, Matt? Willy turn you down?''

"On the contrary, she suddenly became convinced of my integrity, which shook me. I'll have to stop seeing her."

"I thought lawyers, even young ones with ambition, were honest nonplayboy types."

"You are extraordinarily innocent. Young men in any trade or profession are a mixed bag, so to speak. Me, I neither want, nor can I afford, a wife at this stage. Where are you going?"

"Kitchen. I'll cry quietly there."

When she returned with the refreshments and biscuits for Moxie to crunch with his coffee — he liked a saucerful, one sugar and a little cream — she sat down and said, "Models, I understand, do very well. Willy would be an asset rather than a liability."

"I could never bring a bride to the parental mansion. If she were even moderately bright, she'd soon discover she'd settled for second best. Dad's been a catch for a long time. And I wouldn't dream of trying to buy or even rent a house. . . . Hey, what are you doing with the typewriter? A novel? . . . God forbid!''

"I'm just typing for Dr. Carstairs. He's writing a series of articles for medical journals.''

"You certainly lucked out," Matt said admiringly. "This is good coffee. . . . Every woman in town, almost, would give her eyeteeth, if any . . . there'd be a rush for lessons in instant typing, Gregg, and a quick course in medical nomenclature. How often do you see the resident Apollo?''

"He comes by weekends, or has — or I can leave the copy at his house. You certainly make him sound revolting.''

"I don't mean to. Even males, reasonably normal, have to admit he's spectacular. Go ahead and do your stint. Moxie will sleep; I'll sit here and moan.''

"There's no hurry," Maggie said, laughing.

"Do you realize," Matt asked, "now that it's another year, it's practically spring?''

"No.''

"You haven't noticed the days getting longer ever since December twenty-first? No, of course, you wouldn't. You may in February . . . which reminds me, we'll have to clear the calendar for a ski weekend."

"Matt, I couldn't afford it. I've heard what they cost."

"Balderdash, whatever that means. You are kneading a little extra bread — that's with a K and no pun intended. Also it won't be long before you come into your inheritance, just like a Gothic heroine, although a gal who looks less Gothic I can't imagine. What will you do with all your money?"

"Save it for a world cruise or the first commercial flight to the moon."

"Idiot," he said, with affection. "Listen, Maggie, if you're hard up — "

"I am not really. Greg sent me a big Christmas check."

"Which reminds me, I never asked what else Santa brought you — "

"For one thing a robe from Lani, which I can't wear until the next hot spell — not without long johns beneath it, which would destroy the effect. Oh, I had perfume, which I don't use, and other goodies, leis and things."

"You gave those away?"

"No, I gave only those I'd asked my family to send."

"Mrs. Hunt will never recover from hers."

Presently he and Moxie rose and when she went to the door with them, Matt smote her gently on her rear which had almost recovered from the fall. "Stay out of trouble," he advised. "Or if you can't, remember your attorneys. You're entitled to one phone call."

"I'm aware of my rights. For heaven's sake, go home. . . . I'm sorry, Moxie; you can stay as long as you like."

Moxie sighed and, forgivingly, laid his nose on her slipper.

"It's eerie," his owner remarked, "how that dog's taken to you; it's amost an obsession. When I'm out, I think he's more here than at home — providing you're in. I should get him to a shrink. They come now for the four-footed, I hear."

"I suppose they lie on couches and recall their dreams?"

"What else? . . . Think about the ski weekend. We'll rent skis and boots for you."

"Never!"

"Katie or one of the gals can lend you the necessary outer clothing; you have glamorous garments for après ski. You'll enjoy it. Ask Mrs. Carstairs. They go to Clancy's Joint. She's small, Magpie, if chunkier. She'd lend you what you need. She's a generous woman. Incidentally, I'll foot the bill and charge the estate."

"Why are you so good to me?"

"Because I want you to work for me, come summer. I've been asked to run for selectman. We can use typists, receptionists, girls on the phones — all pretty for choice, and with good speaking voices."

"I give up," said Maggie.

"Good. I thought you would. . . . Come on, Moxie, the lady has work to do."

They departed and Maggie returned to the typewriter. A ski weekend might be fun. After all, she didn't even have to put on a pair of skis, much less use them!

On Friday night, Lily Carstairs telephoned to say Alan was at a meeting; could she and Kim drop by and pick up the manuscript of the last article? . . . They came. Maggie offered coffee, which Lily refused, but Kim had a Coke. It so happened that Matt was out of town on a case, so Moxie was standing guard duty.

"He's gentle as a dove," Maggie assured Kim, "unless you tease him, throw things, or threaten me."

Kim favored her with a disdainful look from his mother's eyes set in the little boy face, blunt like hers. He said, "We have a Dane and an Airedale. I know my way around." He fell down on the floor beside Moxie and went into conference.

"Matt Comstock says you and Dr. Carstairs ski," Maggie said.

"Oh, we do. Alan's good; Kim's getting there. I try — I'm still taking lessons. You've never been to Cloud Edge?"

"No. Matt has suggested I go up with him for a weekend."

"We plan a Lincoln's Birthday trip. Fortunately, as Alan isn't a surgeon or a GP or GYN, he can get away."

Maggie said doubtfully, "I have heavy clothes now but not the right kind. I can ask around. I think Katie Palmer skis, or

116

perhaps Amy Irvington — or they used to — "

"I've quantities of clothes," Lily said. "You're welcome to anything — parkas, ski pants, whatever. When Alan was first interested — we were in Maryland and used to fly to Colorado — I depleted the ski shops. We both took lessons. I stayed a willing beginner, he progressed — " She broke off to say thoughtfully, "Odd, isn't it? That is the story of a great many marriages, but in most serious areas. . . . Anyway do take what you need. They won't really fit as I'm pounds heavier and you have a figure, but we're about the same height. I hope you make it February, so we can be there together — we like you so much," she said, with her warm smile.

After they'd gone, Maggie told herself: "That's a lovely woman," and added, "She deserves him."

That year Mr. Lincoln's birthday fell on a Tuesday. Matt could get away for the long weekend, so could the Carstairs; Andrew Comstock was off to visit his sister in Boston and Mrs. Hunt also had

117

plans. Moxie went with Matt and Maggie to Cloud Edge where he was always welcome. He enjoyed the snow and cold and was careful not to run on the beginners' slopes, thus causing disasters.

Maggie had a suitcase full of Lily's expensive gear and said to Matt, "Suppose I ruin something?"

"You won't . . . besides she couldn't care less. Can't you figure it out? All she cares about is her husband and her son, with something pleasant left over for a few friends. I never knew anyone who thought as little of money."

"That's because she has it!"

"It's not always the case, Magpie. If she didn't have a dime over what they'd need — food, shelter, necessities — she still wouldn't care."

"How would you know?"

"Student of human nature. Our office has seen many clients come and go, so have I since I was a kid and used to barge in and take over office-boy duties when it seemed appropriate. We aren't fussy about clients. We have old, young, middle-aged, rich, poor and in between."

"You kill me."

"Why? That is to say, there are times when I could."

"You're so *sure* of yourself," she complained. "It borders on the arrogant."

"Come hear me in court," he said. "I'm sensational. Glad you came along on this trip?"

"Yes, but the driving scares me."

"Clancy's will banish your fears."

The Lodge was on a local mountain — or the nearest thing to local; it was not a very high mountain but perfectly adequate. The weather was fine; there had been recent snow, so the slopes were fine too, with new powder. Clancy didn't need the snow machine and thanked God for it.

Mr. Clancy, the owner, looked like Santa Claus; his son, Ed, was half his width and a third taller. Both were cordial and greeted Maggie as if they'd always known her. Her room, spacious and well heated, looked out on the slopes and was across from Matt's.

They had arrived shortly before a superb sunset. Skiers and observers were coming in from the slopes and Matt said, "Well, tonight we eat, drink and, I hope, make merry. Put on a pretty pants suit or whatever. Not utilitarian. Meet you in the lounge."

The lounge had a four-sided fireplace, a great many sofas, deep chairs, tables and occupants.

None were known to Maggie, but Matt knew half a dozen and by cocktail time they were at a big table and the skiers were talking and someone limped in with a sprained ankle. The Carstairs arrived in time for dinner.

After dinner there was a conversation, also singing and dancing, and an Alpine type of music with Alpine entertainment — or so Maggie judged.

The next day Matt dismissed her from the breakfast table saying, "Go right up and put on your uniform."

"But I've never even — " she began, appealing to Lily Carstairs.

Lily said, smiling, "Try."

"I'm sure you have an aptitude, a natural grace," her husband added.

"He says that to all his patients," Matt told her.

"But I'm not a patient."

"Don't quibble!"

So she went to her room and got into what she thought of, privately, as her finale costume. Looking in the long mirror, she concluded that it became her. Lily had selected the clothes. "Not red," she'd said. "How about this hunter's green?"

Matt hammered at her door. "What's keeping you?" he demanded.

"Vanity. Also the notion that I may be looking at myself for the last time. What happens if you have an accident on top of the mountain?"

"Stretcher, sleds. But you won't be on top."

He looked very well in his skiing outfit. She told him and he said, "I'm not very good, you know. I don't have time. Carstairs now — he's almost professional. Let's go; it's time you met your instructor, Franz. Nice guy. I signed you up before we came."

"I thought you'd teach me."

"Good Lord, no!"

"But instruction must cost an arm

and a leg."

"Without it, perhaps that's what you'd pay. Come on."

Franz was pleasant, moderately young and very skilled. There were a dozen or more others in the class.

When the lesson was over, Maggie wandered with some others into a little chalet-type building from which they could watch other groups on the practice slopes and skiers beyond them. Maggie saw Lily Carstairs now in an advanced class; she saw Kim with his father on one of the higher slopes, moving with no apparent effort.

Matt found her at lunchtime and they walked back to the lodge, Matt carrying their skis.

"Franz said you were a good pupil," he told her. "Did you enjoy it?"

"Yes, but I was scared. There we stood just making gestures, it seemed to me, and every once in a while one of us would fall down, including me. It's absurd."

"You'll learn that one way to fall is to point your skis too close together and then lean backward," he said, laughing. "After lunch we're going to do a little tobogganing with the Carstairs and then a rest and dinner. Tomorrow a sleigh ride.''

At dinner, Alan Carstairs asked, ''You surf, Maggie, don't you?''

They were now at the first-name stage. The Lodge was not a place which encouraged formality.

''Why, yes,'' she said astonished, ''what made you think so?''

''Hawaii,'' he answered, smiling. ''You think of surf riding, swimming, diving, catamarans, canoes and fishing. Also golf and tennis'' — he smiled at his wife — ''and of other things, such as moonlight and stars, flowers and music.''

Maggie felt a little constriction in the region of her heart and thought: I'm homesick.

By the end of the weekend Moxie had fallen in love with Kim.

''Don't be upset,'' Matt consoled Maggie. ''This is man stuff; boys together. He'll always love you.''

Then it was time to go home. Franz was pleased with Maggie's progress. She could stand. She could even essay a few steps.

No one at the Lodge had been seriously hurt on that holiday, a few wrenches, lame backs and one break.

On the way home, Matt asked, "Did you have fun?"

"The most."

"We'll do it again. You're a good sport, Maggie."

She thought: I hope so.

"You're very quiet," he suggested later.

"Just remembering what fun it was," she said quickly. "And I do thank you, Matt."

"A pleasure," he said. "I'm proud of you. I doubt you have even a bruise."

Physically, no; emotionally she was black and blue and her principles were badly sprained. "You can't be in love with Alan Carstairs," she told herself, *"he's married."*

There had been two others prior to this — one a professor at college, the other her first boss at the hospital. The sort of reaction people once called crushes. You simply worshiped from afar. It was natural. Greg had told her so when he'd seen her "mooning around," as he expressed it. He explained it was part of growing up, like falling in love with a motion-picture or television star.

"Boys go through it too," he had assured her. "I started by falling in love with one of my teachers when I was ten. When she left to be married, I was practically suicidal. So believe me, Maggie, you'll recover."

She had; and had then told her stepfather, "From now on in, I run away from, not toward, any married man who attracts me."

Now, "What did you say?" Matt asked. "Either you've taken to muttering or I'm getting deaf — at my age!"

"Nothing," Maggie answered. But she *had* spoken aloud — one word.

"You said something. It sounded like 'pill' — which is interesting. Any passerby could read a number of meanings into that. . . . So, what kind of pill?"

"I must have said *'pilikia'* — without knowing it. For a second I suppose I was back home."

"What does it mean?" he persisted.

"It's just a sort of exclamation like

125

'gosh' or 'heavens to Betsy.' "

"Do they still say that in Hawaii?"

"Well, it's hard to translate."

It wasn't. What Maggie had said merely meant "trouble."

8

There were other weekends and holidays during the long winter that produced sufficient snow to cause the owners of runs and lodgings to dance the Schuplatter, the skiers to rejoice, and orthopedic surgeons to order new cars. Once Maggie went to the Lodge with Matt and his father who, not to her astonishment, was an excellent and properly cautious performer on the packed snow. She herself improved each time but lacked, Matt told her, the necessary abandon to be a real buff, fearless and somewhat demented.

Two or three times the Carstairs took her with them — Matt was away — and Lily had said on the first occasion, "Do come with us. You can go on with your lessons and we'd all love to have you. Kim thinks you are, as he expresses it, 'the living end' . . . and it's fun there, all the people we meet from within and outside of the area. . . ."

Maggie could now afford Franz and her other expenses. Andrew advanced her a monthly sum; she had extra money from the typing stint, her own salary and also her small savings to fall back on. Lily had wished her to be their guest, but she had thanked her and declined, as she also did when she went with Andrew and Matt.

She told Andrew, afterward, "But I do feel guilty spending money on superfluous amusements."

"Nonsense! Hattie would have wished it and it's not a fortune. The Clancy rates are lower than the comparable places around here, which is why you meet so many young people — men and women who work for their livings, as well as college kids, though of course they may be underwritten by indulgent parents. It's good for you to meet people. You're too young to rusticate."

"So Lily Carstairs says, but I know a good many people right now in Little Oxford."

"I think Mrs. Carstairs meant eligible

men. There are damned few of those around the hospital or, for that matter, in our town or those nearby. Most of the males are old, juvenile, or married. Matt tells me, for instance, how eligible I am!"

"You are," Maggie agreed. "And for that matter, so's Matt."

"Not I, my dear. No one has appealed to me as a possible housemate since Matt's mother's death — except Hattie and she wouldn't have me. As for Matt, his self-publicized fun and games with — almost always — quite beautiful, but to me uninteresting, young women does not puzzle me. He's a good deal more ambitious than you'd think — it doesn't show — and utterly opposed, I'm afraid, to being tied down. Which distresses me. I'd like grandchildren before I am gathered to my ancestors."

One weekend was memorable. It came in with a blazing blizzard which kept everyone indoors. Maggie, who was with the Carstairs, complained she ate too much.

"You couldn't even skate," mourned Kim.

There were cards — contract with Alan and Lily and any fourth who'd make up a table. Kim played double solitaire with Maggie. Chess, Maggie played with Alan. She played a creditable game, Greg having taught her. Lily didn't play.

She said, "Alan's kind enough to say I'm intelligent and heaven knows I should know something about mathematics. But the game defeats me. Besides, it makes me nervous. How two people can sit, stare, and not move for what seems hours is beyond me!"

They made it back to Little Oxford behind the ploughs late that Sunday night.

Maggie's skiing may have advanced, but so had her problem. She told herself, looking into her mirror at the flushed cheeks, the tumbled hair — she frequently ran her hands through it, and tugged — and the wide bright eyes, "But I'm not doing any harm!"

Greg had been right. It really was a little like the movie-star syndrome. She simply liked to look at Alan Carstairs, and to listen. He had a good speaking voice —

quiet, deep, sometimes caressive, especially when he spoke to his wife. Also he sang, as Maggie learned, when the après-ski groups gathered.

She spoke to his wife about this and Lily said, "I've tried ever since we were married to get him into a choir — first in Baltimore, then the suburbs, now in Little Oxford. He refuses, although his specialty rarely calls him out on a Sunday. Kim's more amenable. He does sing, but his voice will change and after that we'll see. There's a lot of music in Alan's family. . . . One sister — she died before we'd married — an aunt, a cousin — "

Alan who was present said, laughing, "I cannot imagine myself in a choir; it was also hard for me to imagine Kim."

Kim said, "Well, it's sort of fun."

"I suppose so. I often wish my sister could have had the requisite education. It wasn't possible . . ."

During the lodge visits Maggie learned a good deal about slaloms, schusses, sitzmarks — she made a number of them — what *langläufer* meant and also about snow resistance.

Matt was fascinated. "You talk such a good run, you really don't have to make one — just sit in the lounge, look pretty and talk. I must introduce you to spring skiing, if I can't get up before. Sorry about that, but the law extracts its pound of flesh — I've lost four recently — and justice, which isn't always the same thing, extracts its pint of blood — usually from the heart. I wouldn't dare go near a bloodmobile, I'm too emaciated."

Maggie had learned something beside ski chat. She had learned that being with Alan Carstairs was becoming very pleasurable, and it frightened her. It was like drinking; you could take or leave it, at first, or so you thought.

Being with Lily Carstairs was painful. Maggie liked her so much and admired her even more. In any case, even if she detested her, that would be no excuse. She thought, often: If I could see Greg; if only he'd come here or I could go home.

She saw her friends regularly — lunch, dinner, tea, the occasional party — and Stacy took her to call on Vanessa Steele. Booted, if not spurred, they struggled up the roads which, although ploughed, had ruts and unexpected pitfalls.

Shadow appeared to approve of Maggie.

"See," said Stacy. "He looked you over, purred, and lay down. That's applause! He's really selective, isn't he, Van?"

Vanessa agreed. She said, "He has good taste. . . . I hear you still have a follower," she told Maggie briskly.

"Like Shadow?" Maggie asked, smiling.

"Being willful will not help you," Vanessa said. "Matt Comstock, of course. I've known him off and on since he was a youngster. You could do worse as they say, but as I say it would be better if you didn't try."

Maggie said mildly, "I'm not trying, Mrs. Steele — just playing what field there is."

"Take your time," Stacy advised. "It pays."

Maggie felt a slight chill and the spoon rattled in the saucer as she took her cup of tea from Vanessa's brown hands. Vanessa had strange eyes which shifted color but not direction. You felt she could — almost — read your mind.

133

What had she meant by "You could do worse . . . but it would be better if you didn't try"?

She spoke of a mind reader to Stacy later and Stacy said, "Oh, Van does that quite often. Lee says not; he says she's been around and consequently knows a good deal about people, so it isn't mind reading — just knowledge, not always accurate. Vanessa tends to type people and draw conclusions from their mannerisms, facial expressions, and what she calls give-away gestures. Maybe Lee's right, but I don't believe him a hundred percent."

"I don't either and while I've always liked cats, hers scares me . . . not that I don't find him fascinating."

"Shadow's a con man, a phony, not as black as his coat — have you ever seen a blacker? — or reputation. When you get to know him, he's just another pussycat even if he runs errands and delivers messages."

"Come on!"

"Really. Most cats are intelligent and independent. Shadow isn't the average run-of-the mill kitten. Vanessa brought him up; she's trained him; she's attentive. She talks to him sensibly. Most cat owners don't. They often spoil them of course, but few respect their independence and character, or talk to them, man-to-man."

"Vanessa's theory?"

"Certainly. She swears she'll write the definitive cat book — not about breeds, diets, or illnesses but psychology."

"I must tell Moxie; he'll expect Matt to do a biography."

"Why not you? You see him almost as much as Matt does."

"That's true. Matt's away a lot and sometimes, even here, he goes places where a four-foot can't, so Moxie comes padding down to me for consolation and a healthful goodie. . . . Has Matt pressed you into service for his campaign? I suppose he'll start turning up at gatherings by spring, and then have some sort of campaign headquarters."

"Oh, yes, he spoke to us both. I don't believe him. Why would he involve himself in small-town politics other than, perhaps, backing someone else?"

"It's one way to the state legislature, which becomes a way to Washington —

Congress, Senate — or do you think he'd settle for governor? He has a lot of sound ideas and not just for Little Oxford, I think."

Stacy shrugged. "I don't really understand ambitious people. Oh, I always wanted to paint better, but that's about it."

"That's all?"

"Well, a baby or two, and maybe an occasional holiday in Greece."

Also to be loved and to love for the rest of her life, she thought, although she didn't say it.

"What about Lee?"

"Well, he's already recognized and not just in this state. He's really a great architect," Stacy answered, smiling.

Afterward, Maggie reflected upon the conversation — cats to dogs to politics to ambition. She thought: It must be pretty special to be that proud of your guy and to believe him to be important, not only to you, but to his times. I suppose Lily feels the same way. Alan's a young man but well known in his field; he lectures, he teaches and writes papers.

Washington's Birthday was observed that year on a Monday so the Country Club did not have its annual dance that weekend. It would have been in competition with ski resorts nearby or just a plane flight away. There wouldn't have been many celebrants except the mature — heaven forbid the Country Club would think of members as elderly. There were a few exceptions as, for instance, Andrew Comstock and Bing Irvington, who sometimes found their way down the slopes, but, the committee on arrangements had thought, these two had always been somewhat eccentric, if not as eccentric as Jeremy Palmer, who had not joined until last fall. They'd made room for him and his wife, because of her really. She was very active in real estate and Emily Warner's agency had been known to supply a good many suitable and affluent new residents — like the Carstairs and, of course, the Ross Camerons and others.

So the dance was held on the following Saturday, on a sleety, cold, miserable night. It was well attended, however, and members and their guests slid and swore their way to dining and dancing.

Maggie went with Andrew and Matt; Moxie anguished at home. She asked Matt, "What happened to Willy? I told your father that if you brought her, I could scare up — if not away — an extra man. I've actually met a few."

"Extraordinary girl," Matt mourned, as they sat in the comfortable cocktail lounge. "She fell in love with a jazz pianist; he's about five foot six. I'll never understand women."

"They don't want to be understood," his father consoled him. "Men don't, either. . . . Hey, there's Bing."

Everyone was there: both sets of Irvingtons; the Palmers, Jeremy looking attractively reluctant; the Osbornes; the Carstairs. People table-hopped and danced and Maggie danced once with Alan Carstairs.

He said, "We hope you missed us over the last weekend. We'd thought about going to the Lodge —"

"Of course. Lily said when she called that you all had to go to Baltimore."

"Her last remaining maiden aunt — she's the youngest. Kim was extremely bored but well behaved. He doesn't see her often. Actually she's a rather splendid old girl. I'm very fond of her. Every so often she gets a spell of I-might-die-tomorrows, and telephones Lily. . . . You're looking well and, as usual, very pretty. If all my female patients were like you, I'd have to give up my practice. No allergies and not a blemish."

"I was brought up on *poi,*" said Maggie.

"Seriously, how's the work going?"

"Fine. They're awfully busy at the hospital, of course, and our office is humming."

"I don't get up there much," he said. "Now and then, as you know, I bring someone in for tests. Occasionally, there's a very ill patient and it takes time to determine why. The bulk of the practice comes to my office. I'll be doing a few lectures, in the spring. I thought possibly you could find the time to type up some notes."

"I'd be glad to."

She felt dizzy and prayed that it wouldn't

show. She thought: But this is ridiculous!

She said, "I'm trying to persuade my stepsister to fly over and visit me when it gets warm. She's never been as far north. I wouldn't rate a vacation so soon, but I'm sure all my friends would look after her."

"Is she anything like you?"

"She couldn't be. I was three when her father married my mother. She was a little older. And she's beautiful."

"Well —" he began.

"But she interrupted, "Don't bother to say it," she told him, "and wait 'til you see Lani. She's tall and dark, with dark eyes. Matt's impressed. I have two photographs and a lot of snapshots."

"I'm not very susceptible," said her partner. "Well, the music's stopped. I see Bing persuaded Lily . . . she doesn't really like dancing, although she dances very well."

The sleet storm had abated, but people began going home earlier than usual.

"You're very quiet, Maggie," Matt remarked.

She yawned with ostentation. "Sleepy . . . but it was a lovely evening."

Matt said, "I'll have to stop attending these clambakes. The females are either adolescent, or home from college or married. What a town! Practically no homegrown eligibles."

"Me," Maggie reminded him with dignity.

"You're a transplant. Besides you're not my type."

Andrew roused himself. He said, "Pay him no mind, although I'm sure you're not crushed. Anything short of a fright wig and bad legs is his type. I don't know where he gets this tendency. . . . And besides," he told his son, "you don't think any woman's eligible in the standard sense of the word."

"I'm taking the Fifth," Matt told him.

When they reached Maggie's, he left his father in the car. He said, "We may not make it up the hill, Dad. If you hear a crash, come running. . . . I think you're making a mistake, Maggie."

"About what?"

"Not what, whom."

Maggie was very still, inside and out. She could see her breath on the air; she heard particles of ice falling from the

141

trees. "I don't know what you mean," she said.

"Yes, you do; you aren't stupid. I've seen Dr. Apollo's effect on gals before. All losers, Maggie, believe me."

"Shall we discuss this another time?" she asked politely. "I'm freezing."

"I'll take you to dinner, say Thursday, to a nice, dark pleasant place where you can cry on my shoulder. . . . Give me your key."

She did. He opened the door, and she closed it — very hard — from the other side.

"And what was that?" asked Andrew, when Matt returned to the car.

"Just Maggie, reverberating."

"Fine night for a disagreement. Hope it didn't make you nervous. Thank God we haven't far to go. . . . Matt, it's none of your business."

The car skidded slightly. Matt swore.

"What isn't?"

"Maggie's starry eyes. Good Lord, Matt, the man can't help his appearance! I watched him dancing with Maggie and others, including his wife. I noticed she danced only with him, except once with Bing. Great post, the side lines; one becomes an observer. All Dr. Carstairs's partners were starry-eyed, including his wife, who is a very nice woman. . . . Well, here we are," he said unnecessarily.

Later, as they went upstairs to their bedrooms, Andrew advised, "Don't worry about Maggie."

"I don't."

"Look, despite all this dovecote fluttering, nothing will come of it. I doubt if anyone's hurt except in pride or vanity. Most women have their share. Little Oxford's self-elected sirens, for instance. They've all tried."

"How do you know so much?"

"Observation. Also, people talk more than they realize," Andrew answered gravely.

9

Maggie blew into the coffee shop like a bright autumn leaf, or bird. She'd experienced a somewhat upsetting morning. Mr. Davis had kept his amiable cool, but Mrs. Cromwell had been alternately flushed and wan; her usually brushed and polished hair had not only been ruffled but had looked as if it stood on end. Things had just not Gone Well, as often happens in any institution however well run and regulated. Maggie pieced together what she knew officially, and what had filtered through as rumor.

Two malpractice suits were pending, which is not unusual; a feud had started to build between a new surgeon and one of the older men; there was trouble in the kitchen; one excellent charge nurse would be leaving to be married and another, having had a slight disagreement with the head of the nursing school, had just resigned. In short, a routine-type but emotionally charged day in any good-sized hospital; people took sides. In addition, an intern had been mugged on a dark side street during his night off and was now in the intensive care unit, and an ambulance driver had died early that morning in his car on his way to work.

Never a dull moment, Maggie thought.

"Hi," said a pretty volunteer, shortly after Maggie had found a small table. "What's it to be?"

"Quail on toast for openers?" Maggie suggested.

"Never touch 'em; besides we're sold out. Settle for ham on rye?"

"Why not? Also coffee."

"You drink too much coffee," Alan Carstairs remarked critically, materializing beside her, as the volunteer departed. "Mind if I sit down?"

"No, I'd love it," Maggie said truthfully. "This hasn't been my day and I need a shoulder to cry on."

"Consider it offered." He raised a finger and another volunteer promptly deserted the table she was about to wait on, barreled over, and inquired soulfully, "What may I do for you, Doctor?"

"Just coffee," he told her, smiling, "black."

"You probably drink too much yourself," Maggie said.

He shook his head. "Lily won't let me. Now and then I escape. I'm sorry we didn't make the projected weekend. We all missed you. Kim puts you in a special category, slightly above all women except his mother, and a couple of cousins."

"Where do you place?"

"A throne-step below Lily but above Tom Seaver."

"What brings you here today, Alan? I seldom see you around."

"Staff meeting."

Her lunch arrived and shortly after, Alan's coffee.

"It's too hot," he said.

"A good fault," Maggie reminded him.

"What's the old saying about coffee, that it should be as strong as jealousy, hot as hell, sweet as love?" He shook his head, "I've forgotten. What happened to disturb you today?''

''Well,'' Maggie said, ''some of it's just rumor.''

''I've heard it,'' he assured her. ''I've been to a staff meeting, remember, and that tends to break up in little groups afterward.'' He looked at the clock on the coffee-shop wall. ''I'll be late to lunch,'' he said, ''and after lunch, office hours. Be seeing you.''

He rose, sketched a salute and walked toward the door. Maggie watched him, as did a number of other people. Those who knew him — and not many did — spoke; the others just watched.

The adjective ''beautiful'' was for a long time rarely applied to a man — any other male animal, yes — but lately it has come into use. In Alan Carstairs's case, no one hearing it would laugh or raise an eyebrow, and many thought privately or aloud, if there were a handsomer man, he — or she — had never seen him.

When the day was over, Maggie was glad to head for the parking area. Visitors were hurrying out; eveyone's breath smoked in the still air. It was bitterly cold, but

February is short and it was almost over.

The last time Maggie had seen Vanessa Steele, who had stopped in with Shadow, Vanessa had said, "I'm too old for cold weather. Now and then I think I'd like to go south — south of France or Italy — Greece, perhaps." She was smoking one of her thin cigars and watching Shadow prowl about the room, his tail enormous. "He smells dog," she diagnosed. "Matt's, I presume?"

Maggie had agreed.

"Don't make a federal case of it," Vanessa admonished her cat, "not even a production. You rather like Moxie. As dogs go, he's harmless, if not as enchanting as Oscar. . . . I don't like February," she went on, "but you can look ahead. Remember groundhog day? Not a shadow to be seen, at least in this area. It snowed a foot."

Now after Washington's Birthday, it was cold, and the thick ice held. All told it had been a colder and snowier winter than Little Oxford had had in recent years. Flakes kept drifting down, out of the blue sometimes, and people who read almanacs and newspapers asked gloomily, "Well,

148

how about March and the blizzard of '88?''

That evening after supper Moxie knocked on the door and was admitted, followed by his alleged master.

"We were strolling past," Matt explained, "and Moxie wondered how you were, so I said, 'We'll ask. . . .' I'm tired." He collapsed in the nearest suitable chair and Moxie took to the floor beside him. "Stay us with flagons, Maggie, I beseech you."

"I'm fresh out of flagons, dear."

"Don't be familiar; I've given you no encouragement. How about Scotch?"

"Cupboard. The bottle your father gave me, so I could cater to his, and your, inexplicable taste. Go get it."

"No one ever waits on me, except Mrs. Hunt, and that's only because she's really in love with my father. I have yet to meet a girl who would rush to do my slightest bidding. She doesn't even have to be beautiful," he said, "just patient, ready and willing."

"I doubt the paragon exists."

"You're very unfeeling. . . . Stay with her, Moxie, but don't let her influence you.

. . . May I bring you something, Maggie?"
he asked politely.

"Coffee on the pilot light; it must still be
hot."

When he brought his glass, he brought
her cup. "You drink too much coffee," he
informed her.

"So Alan suggested, at lunch."

"Lunch?" Matt's shaggy eyebrows
climbed. "Not, I trust, a tryst? Try to say
that fast," he suggested, pleased with
himself.

"Don't be absurd," Maggie counseled
crossly. "I was ordering a sandwich and
java in the coffee shop. He came by, said I
probably drank too much coffee, ordered
some himself and left most of it as he had
to go home for lunch."

"Everyone who works in a hospital
drinks too much coffee. I once knew a
nurse, quite well. She could reduce a fever
— even create one — but I couldn't watch
her consume fourteen to sixteen cups a
day, as she did, one weekend when we
happened to meet in Manchester."

"Is she still at the hospital?"

"She never was. I go in for imports and

always steer clear of local girls."

"Including me?" asked Maggie, making an affronted face.

"You're not local, Magpie. And some people have lived here for sixty years and still aren't. Some, like Vanessa, become local on the the day they become residents. Of course, you have to remember, she's a witch. Others, like Stacy Osborne, become local through marriage. But natives are different. They were born here; sometimes their fathers before them; their grandfathers, like me, Ben and others."

"Incredible," Maggie said. "Sounds like England when, as I recall from novels, not everyone in a county was County with a capital C. Actually, peasant blood would do Little Oxford good; also a large amount of other races. . . . Hey, what about Rosie Niles?"

"Born here, local, with a touch of native. Now take the Carstairs. They'd never make it — however handsome — that's Alan — delightful and rich — that's Lily — even though they are assets to the community and he's a very good man in his field."

"I don't get it. Why?"

"Don't bridle. I don't know. They'll never know. It isn't that anyone is hostile; it's simply that they're aliens. Lily Carstairs is, I suspect, one of the few really tremendous women I've ever known."

"How can you endure living here?"

"Your Aunt Hattie lived here all her life, and her parents."

"Ha!" said Maggie, in triumph. "That makes me a native. Mother, grandaunt, grandparents —"

"Of course, but by inheritance. You weren't born here."

"I don't see how Aunt Hattie lived here either. No wonder she escaped now and then."

"Lots of us escape occasionally, when we can afford it. Your aunt loved this place; so do you."

"In a way," she admitted, "but against my principles. Little Oxford is ultra-snob. It goes beyond ordinary snobbery — status, money, even family. It's . . . I can't find the right word."

"Provincial," he supplied.

"You said it, I didn't."

"Actually a highly sophisticated — and excuse my use of the adjective; it's been incorrectly used for so many years, it's common usage — as I was saying, a highly sophisticated small town is always provincial. Regard those poor devils, the property owner-commuters. They stumble off to their offices in a senile train or perilous automobile; they work like crazy; they scream over telephones; they eat interminable lunches, though often on a diet; and limply return to their little gray home in the East, two to twenty acres and a swimming pool, or maybe just to an elegant condominium, for, as they tell everyone, they are simple country folk. Next day it begins all over again. Leave us not discuss weekends. As for those of us who work as well as live here, we too are provincial but right from the ancestral mold."

Moxie rose, stretched, wandered over to Maggie, put his beautiful head upon her knee and stood there looking wistful, and making small apologetic sounds.

"What's wrong, Moxie?" she asked.

"Past your bedtime?"

"He wants out," Matt interpreted, "also he's saying good night and thanking you for a restful evening. I shall too." He loped over, hauled her to her feet and kissed her firmly but without urgency. " 'Bye," he said. "Hang loose."

Maggie went upstairs and to bed, after locking up. She was highly indignant. When a man kissed her, whether or not she enjoyed it, she preferred a less impersonal attitude. Matt might as well have been kissing Aunt Hattie, she thought, and then reflected: Perhaps he had been.

But she was sorry he'd gone; she wished he and Moxie had stayed a little longer. She knew she couldn't sleep, and a book wouldn't help; neither would radio or TV. She was forced to think about Alan Carstairs, calmly and dispassionately. So, what was he? A pleasant, very attractive man and, she assumed, a good friend once you came to know him more than superficially. And she didn't.

He was also Lily's husband and she liked Lily. He was Kim's father, and she liked Kim, not only as a ten-year-old kid

154

but as a person.

She thought: I don't have to stay here. As soon as everything is settled, Andrew and Katie can sell the house, land, car and everything else. I can go home and get a job. I can live in Honolulu or Hilo.

She loved Greg and Lani, but she didn't want to live with them. She'd become accustomed to her own house. Lani would be mistress in Greg's house until she married, and while Maggie'd been free enough in the California apartment, she'd shared it.

She thought: I don't want to share *anything*.

Also she didn't want to leave what she had here: the house, which was growing like a carapace around her, a solid shell of security, with as much privacy as she wanted; the house in which her grandparents had lived, in which her mother had grown up, and in which her grandaunt had been born and died. She liked it here in her inherited shell. She liked her work at the hospital and the friends she had made.

She switched on the light and sat up. She

shivered. The wind was busy and cold, northwest. She wished she'd taken up smoking. But when she was fourteen she'd promised Greg that she wouldn't, and the few times she'd broken her promise, she'd felt it wasn't worth it. Vanessa . . . now when she couldn't sleep, did she smoke her cigars?

She got up and into a robe, went downstairs to heat a glass of milk with Greg's remedy, a splash of rum, found a book that might do.

When finally she slept, she did not dream of her ancestors, or Alan Carstairs or anyone she knew in Little Oxford or of Little Oxford. She dreamed of herself. She saw herself clearly, a sixteen-year-old girl, shivering in a warm and fragrant breeze on a sunny *lanai,* crying her eyes out because a Navy pilot who had kissed her once and gone away had never come back. . . . And when she woke, her face was wet.

She hadn't thought of him in years; she hadn't been in love with him, though she slipped easily in and out of love. She had seen him just a few times and had mourned his descent into the sea as had a dozen other girls.

Frustration, she decided, over her breakfast coffee; frustration and shock. I hardly knew Don. I'd never known anyone that young who had died. I was sixteen and I wouldn't see him again and for a little while after, every time anyone wore a carnation lei, I thought of him.

March came in brisk, windy, cold. When it rained, it rained hard; when it cleared, bits of bright blue sky grew in the puddles. Easter was early that year and it snowed. Maggie spent it with Katie and Jeremy. Jeremy had to be ploughed out to come fetch her for the Easter service and take her back to his house. She'd been ploughed out too — Matt had seen to that.

"Where are the Carstairs, I wonder?" said Katie. "I didn't see them in church. Unlike most doctors he usually gets there with Lily, and Kim's in the choir. What a great kid. I hope our junior is just like him."

"Genetically impossible," said Jeremy, "and don't call him junior."

"Nanny," said Katie, "refers to him as the young master."

"Where is there lots of snow?" Maggie asked.

They regarded her with anxiety.

"Antarctic," Jeremy ventured. "Alaska. Thinking of a trip?"

"Wherever it is, they're there. Lily and Kim came to see me a week or so ago. Seems he wanted a ski vacation. Colorado was out of the question, to his regret, but Lily said something about going north, where there's snow — I'm not sure where — and Kim said I should come along. I told him I had Easter engagements, which I did — the Osbornes last night, with Matt — "

"I asked Matt today," Katie said, "as his father had to go south — sick client, I believe."

"I know. Matt had another date. Anyway the Carstairs are on some distant slopes."

Lily had asked warmly, "Why don't you come? We'd all love to have you," and when she'd said again that she couldn't, Kim had remarked simply, "Rats."

His mother objected mildly, "Revolting expression," she said.

Kim apologized. "Sorry, Mom. How about shucks?"

Shucks was all right.

"I like the Carstairs," Katie said, "and of course feel slightly superior as they are more Johnnie-come-lately than we are. However, Jeremy has a slight edge, being related to Jessica Banks."

"But she wasn't born here," Maggie reminded her.

"That's right and neither was Gordon. It's heartening to remember how many babies *are* — every year, including our pride and joy. Someday everyone will be native."

"Not as long as people from the outside world keep on discovering our quaint village," Jeremy said.

"To return to the Carstairs," Katie remarked, "everyone likes them, but no one seems to know them well."

"They're very private people," Jeremy said, "and they have a count against them."

"You can't mean money," Katie told him exasperated. "The town's loaded. Look at your old war buddy —"

"Please," said Jeremy plaintively.

"I mean Cam," Katie went on, "and Rosie Niles and a hundred more, to say nothing of the descendants of settlers who hung on to the land and then the developers when the heirs sold. Little Oxford accepts the fact that real estate has soared into the wild blue yonder and that many commuters command exorbitant salaries even in these uncertain times. Look at the hopeful brokerage agencies here and in nearby towns, Jeremy. The income per capita is the highest in the county and the county ranks pretty high — so who can look askance at the Carstairs' solvency?"

"No one."

"Then what are your absurd counts against them?"

"Not mine, darling, and nothing tangible. No one has grounds for unpleasant speculations and there's no murky past catching up, as has sometimes happened. No one thinks anything momentous. Lily is a philanthropist; she's given a very agreeable sum to our hospital and to local and state charities. Alan put himself through medical school, which is never easy; ask Bing, he'll tell you about his father. No one, except possibly unmarried females — my apologies, Maggie — holds it against Lily that she's older than her husband and married him when he was a struggling resident."

"Who told you that?"

"I'm sure you did. Anyway, people talk — at hairdressers', I understand; in bookshops, I know. Bookshops are a little like clubs. The habitués come in, gather in little murmuring, exclaiming, even mewing knots, and talk. I've often thought I should serve coffee." He rose and crossed the room to pick up his son. "Wait until you're a bookseller," he warned his amiable offspring.

"You haven't explained anything," Katie said.

"Oh, but I have . . . did sometime back. The Carstairs are private people. They are friendly and charming, but reticent; and reticent newcomers are always suspect."

"This," Maggie said, "is a crazy place."

"No more lunatic than any other, no matter how big or small," Jeremy said. "As every place is inhabited by people."

10

On Monday morning, the telephone woke Maggie from the sort of sleep which tells you it's time to get up, but not quite.

She sat up and reached for the instrument which she'd had moved into her bedroom. "Yes?" she said.

"Maggie," Amy Irvington said, "I'm sorry to call so early, but I thought you'd want to know before you listen to local radio or go to work."

Maggie's heart accelerated. "Know what?"

"Kim was killed yesterday in a skiing accident." Amy's voice roughened. "The poor kid!" she said, and then, "Alan telephoned Ben, also Jim Hutchinson. They're chartering a plane and flying up — they've already gone. . . . Are you still there, Maggie?"

"Yes. Dear God, how incredibly

terrible! What happened. Why?''

''I don't know why,'' Amy said. ''Who would? No one, not even Jim Hutchinson or Gordon Banks or the greatest clergyman who ever lived. I don't even know exactly what happened. I'll get back to you when I know more. You'll hear all sorts of explanations and speculations, I suppose. Better wait. Ben will know. 'Bye.''

Maggie sat on the bed and thought about the friendly, eager, vital ten-year-old, who looked like his mother but stood as his father did and had his father's dark, thick hair. As she thought of what Alan had once said — that Kim had put her in a special category — tears ran down her cheeks and she felt sick.

When she reached the hospital, everyone seemed to know, which was only natural. Bing was taking Ben's patients and she met him in a corridor on her way to deliver a report.

''You've heard,'' he began.

''Amy called me, Dr. Bing. Is there anything I can do?''

''No dear,'' he answered in his

concerned way. "Just pray. . . . I've offered this advice to numerous people, but one can't write a prescription for it. Some have taken it. I'm sure Amy will be in touch with you when we know more."

Maggie survived the day, the stunned faces, the speculations, and went home to find Moxie and Matt waiting for her.

"Have you heard?" she asked.

"Oh, yes. . . . We came to take you to supper."

"It's good of you," Maggie said, "but I don't think I can."

"You can. This has been a shock to you as it has to everyone who knows the Carstairs. If you stay here, you won't eat. I'm going to take you home to Dad and Mrs. Hunt."

"Then let me wash up," she said, and went off obediently.

Andrew was grave, Mrs. Hunt horrified, and Maggie said during dinner, "Amy didn't phone again."

"Perhaps she didn't know anything more," Matt suggested. "I'll call her."

He did so while they were having coffee

and returned to report.

"Freak accident. Kim's parents were together on another slope. He was skiing with some kids around his age, all proficient and in no need of an instructor. Alan and Lily were to meet him later in the afternoon. There was a sudden predicted storm, also ice beneath the snow. Kim fell ... there was a tree — " he said and stopped.

"No unnecessary details," his father warned, watching Maggie's face.

Matt said, "I'm sorry. ... Anyway they'll be back tomorrow. We won't know more for a while."

When they did, it was only that the services were to be completely private; just Kim's parents and Jim Hutchinson. Alan had arranged for a dermatologist in Deeport to cover his practice and for Dr. Murphy, who specialized in allergy at the hospital, to see the others.

Everyone had been more than kind. The Carstairs' house was full of flowers, as there were to be none at the services except those Lily herself had ordered. She made a list of the givers and then sent the multitude of spring arrangements to a nursing home. And sent word to her friends that as soon as she could see them, she hoped they'd come.

But not before she had flown to Baltimore to talk to her grieving aunt and returned.

Maggie went to see Lily on a Saturday. Amy had been, Letty and others, including Bing, Matt and his father. Maggie was almost afraid to go in, and shrank from it, but Lily came to meet her with the familiar warmth, the transforming smile and also with complete composure.

She said, "As I wrote you — the flowers were lovely."

Maggie's mouth shook. She made a valiant attempt. "I don't know how — " she began.

"Don't try. Kim was very fond of you," Lily said, "so, you're special to us too."

She looked old and ravaged, but her hand was steady pouring tea, and she said, when Maggie made a move to go, "Alan should be home any moment. I'm sure he'll want to see you." Her usually expressive eyes were empty as last year's nest as she added, "He can't accept this. I can't either, so we're not much help to each other. And you see" — and now there was expression in her eyes, resentful and bitter — "I can't have another child."

Maggie rose and went over to her. She knelt down and put her arms around her and Lily stayed in them, quiet and unyielding. So Alan found them when he came in.

"She won't talk anymore," Maggie whispered.

"No." He helped Maggie to her feet. He looked, she thought, more damaged than Lily. "Don't cry," he said gently, "She'll be all right. Ben's coming tonight. He's been of enormous help. You all have."

He picked his wife up. "I'll take her upstairs," he said.

Half-blind, Maggie found her way out, got into her car and, sitting there, spoke aloud: "It's so dreadful that they can't help each other."

April, cold and wet, became early May, also wet, if not cold. People who knew the Carstairs best still spoke of their tragedy, looked for and did not find Kim's young face in the choir, but most people, who had known them only slightly — by name or by sight — forgot, as people do. No one can dwell forever on the tragedy that is someone else's. Kim's schoolmates and his teachers mourned, but school went on.

Lily established a foundation. Andrew and Matt set it up for her, and Maggie asked, "Can anyone contribute?"

"Oh, yes," Andrew said. "It's a scholarship project because, Lily told us, Kim won't be able to go to college, but other boys will. However, there's to be no public announcement or appeal."

"I've seen Lily only once,' Maggie said. "I don't know what she does with her time."

"Reads, I imagine," Matt said. "Listens to music, writes letters, goes on walks — I've met her, in the rain, alone, with Kim's dog beside her."

Andrew said, "Maggie, there's no cure, not even time. Time simply scars — and scars never quite stop hurting."

"I'm sorry for Alan," Matt said suddenly.

His father looked at him mildly surprised. "He has his work — " he began.

"Damned little else," Matt said.

It was shortly after that Alan telephoned Maggie. "Are you going to be home this evening?" he asked. "Lily's tired; she wants to go to bed. I'd like to come by, if I may, and just talk?"

He came and brought a notebook. "I've been doing some work," he said. "I've set myself a little research job — and thought you might type up the notes — but that's not entirely why I came." He looked around. "This is such a good house, isn't it? It's always as though someone you like has just left the room. Our house," he added, "is empty, even when we're in it." He walked about, his hands in his pockets. He said, "I wish I were a surgeon or an overworked general practitioner or maybe a guy in a factory coming home at night, to the mortgage and a leaky roof."

Maggie, sitting with her feet drawn up under her, said nothing. She just sat and watched him.

He finally sat down saying, "What I do I do very well and someday I hope I'll contribute something of value. But I don't have the day-by-day, hour-by-hour anxiety and responsibility of the surgeon, the cardiologist, the internist. I don't have the preoccuptation and the worry. . . . I suppose this sounds a little insane."

"No."

"Lily," he said, "is very kind, but she simply isn't there, Maggie. I've lost her. I've lost them both."

"I'm sure you're wrong. She just has to be given time, Alan."

"Ben says that, Bing says it, and I know it. But how much time is there for any of us?" he asked harshly. He stopped and added painfully, "I've no right burdening you — I told Lily so."

"Lily?"

"Why yes," he said. "I suppose she grew tired of seeing me prowl around — because I do, I've moved out of our room — and she said, after dinner, 'Why don't you go to see Maggie? She'll do you good.' She said the same about Amy and Ben."

He rose and went to the door. He said, "I'll walk awhile, I guess, and then go home in case Lily needs me. She hasn't, you know. I thought maybe she would at first and then afterward . . . but she still doesn't. It's lonely."

As Maggie followed him to the door, he asked, "May I come again? You can always throw me out."

She answered, her heart heavy with compassion, "Of course, whenever you like — to talk or not talk as you please."

He bent and kissed her cheek. He said, "Thank you, Maggie."

After that he came often: once to pick up the typed notes; again to bring more; other times, empty-handed.

Matt said one evening, "Moxie and I have wanted to come see you or take you out riding on nights it didn't rain and on Sundays when I've been around . . . but you've been . . . busy."

"Alan comes often," she acknowledged, "stays awhile and goes. Matt, I'm so sorry for him."

"Not for Lily?"

"Of course. She called recently so I went around to see her and she thanked me."

"For what?"

"She told Alan to come here in

171

the first place."

"So I gathered."

"What's that supposed to mean?" she asked, angered.

"Just what I said. Maggie, don't get in over your little red head. . . . When's your stepsister coming?"

"Early next month. She's going to a classmate's wedding in Georgia; she'll come on from there."

"If she looks like her pictures," Matt said, "we'll hang out the banners and break out the band."

They were having coffee at the kitchen table. The warm damp-scented wind twitched the curtains at the open windows and Maggie said, "If it doesn't stop raining soon, all the lilacs will be gone."

"Your aunt set great store by them. . . . You haven't told me about Lani. Does she really look like her photographs?"

"Better — fabulous. Black shining hair to below her waist; she won't cut it. Big, dark eyes — a figure to dream about. I envy her."

"Her appearance?"

"No, her Hawaiian blood. I thought I told

you her grandmother was half-Hawaiian."

"No. . . . Is Lani tall?"

"Taller than I."

"Good. While you're at work, I'll take her around and show her the countryside."

"You'll be working too."

"She might like to drive up to the Capitol and, unless she's a very frivolous girl, could just enjoy hearing me speak my piece. I'll show her our makeshift headquarters in town too. That should impress her."

"I don't think so. Lani has relatives in the legislature at home, and one in the United States Congress," said Maggie loftily. "I knew her grandmother. She died sometime after Greg married my mother. She was the most beautiful old woman I've ever seen. Stroke out 'old,' — just leave 'the most beautiful.' Lani's mother too, from her pictures. She died in childbirth, so Lani never saw her."

"I'll try to clear my calendar," he said generously, "as New England blood is missionary blood."

"Not anymore," said Maggie.

Later, as she was getting ready for bed,

Alan rang the bell. She came downstairs in robe and slippers and admitted him, startled.

"You scared me. I always think of telegrams."

"They don't deliver them anymore, or not as they used to. I apologize for frightening you. I've been walking around for some time, aimlessly, and then, when I passed here, I saw the lights upstairs and turned back."

"Come in," she said and tugged at his arm. He smiled a very little, she was so small and earnest. "Take your things off; you're wet. Please, Alan, you'll catch cold. . . . Sit down and I'll get you something. A drink or coffee or both?"

He said absently, "I don't want anything, thank you." He was sitting hunched forward, his hands clasped between his knees. "I don't mean to sound abrupt, but I've consumed too much coffee these past weeks and more whiskey than's good for anyone — after hours," he added.

She said lightly, sitting down opposite, her curly hair ruffled and her cheeks pink, "At the hospital they talk of building an ark."

He did not answer. And she asked, "Is there something especially wrong, Alan?"

"No . . . yes. Lily won't let me near her, Maggie, not close. I thought last night — and it wasn't the first time — that we could comfort each other. Isn't that what closeness is — when you love each other — not just happiness but comfort?"

"Alan, she'll understand. Things will be all right."

"You don't understand. She permits me to be physically close, but she isn't there." He paused, and then said, "You can pay women for that, but most of them try to pretend."

Maggie was scarlet. She hated sitting there hearing, listening. "I'm sorry — " she began, but he rose, came over, pulled her to her feet and kissed her.

Despite her instinctive response, she thought: But he isn't kissing *me* — not really.

"Please let me go," she said.

He released her instantly, and she moved away to stand beside her chair. "It won't do," she said. "No one replaces anyone, not in the way you want."

"I suppose not," he said. "I'm sorry."

He was gone almost at once, and as Maggie went up to bed she thought: What harm would it have done? It wouldn't have hurt Lily. I don't think anything can ever hurt her again. It wouldn't have hurt Alan — oh, I suppose, the usual guilt, but men get over that. The only person it would hurt is me, she thought, lying there in the warm darkness. And how much would that matter?

The damp breeze blew in, and the lilac scent. Aunt Hattie's lilacs. "If Aunt Hattie were here she'd shake me until my teeth rattled. But this is another time," she said in her mind. "Things have changed, are changing, they'd changed long before she died."

She wished Lani were with her. Maggie had always gone to her stepsister or to Greg with her problems. But not Greg now, she thought. Just Lani.

11

Maggie had just gotten into her car the next afternoon when Alan Carstairs, walking across the parking lot, waved, came over and put his head in at the driver's window. He said, "I must talk with you, Maggie. May I follow you home and come in for a few moments?"

She thought: He looks dreadful; there's no reason why he shouldn't. . . . No. I'll say no. . . .

"I suppose so," she said, "but honestly, it doesn't make sense."

People were coming into the parking lot, talking, calling to one another. He said, "Let's go on. We can argue on your doorstep."

He doesn't want to attract attention, she thought. I don't blame him. I don't want to either.

She drove home, taking corners a little

recklessly, deeply disturbed and uncertain, except in one department. She was still angry. Reaching the house, she went in immediately and he followed.

Once inside, she said, "This is ridiculous, Alan."

"I know." He didn't sit down, he stood. He said, "First, I apologize for last night. It won't happen again. And I'll try to explain. I was lonely. I knew you liked me as you liked us all. I haven't made close friends here, nor has Lily. Only Kim made friends wherever he went — and in ten minutes.

"Lily has always kept herself to herself. On the surface, she is as she was brought up to be — gracious and charming. I don't suppose she's ever had a close friend really. Nor have I. Perhaps that's one reason why, when we came to know each other, it seemed enough for both of us. Each other and then enough to share with Kim.

"Fathers aren't as a rule born to parenthood. Most women are — or were. Lily didn't believe she'd ever have a child. Several excellent specialists had told her it was unlikely. She miscarried twice and was very ill. She was closer to dying than living when Kim was born, which is another reason why her life revolved about him from the first time she was allowed to see him.

"I know that shutting herself away from me, as she has, physically and emotionally, is, under the circumstances, to be expected. I know if I am patient, if I wait it out, things will be, if not all right, at least better. But I get desperate to talk with and to be with someone."

"There must be others — " Maggie began.

"No. My parents worked very hard all their lives; they scratched out a living and managed high-school educations for their children. The family name was unpronounceable and unspellable as many East European surnames are. My father had it legally changed to Carstairs with no difficulty. We were six children — I was the youngest; two are dead, the others have scattered. I have two brothers, one sister, also nephews and nieces whom I never see. I worked my way through the university and medical school. I didn't have time for friends or enough money for an occasional night on the town or to stand someone a drink — "

"Why are you telling me this?"

"I'd like you to know. . . . You can sell blood, you can work as an orderly, you can do a hundred things if you make up your mind and forget your body — oh, there are always willing girls," he said, "but I mean forget it in a real sense, except to try to eat as well as possible — which wasn't easy — to sleep when you can, and to do hard labor when it pays, and to remember that's all you have; that and your mind to get you to where you want to go. But I couldn't even try to make friends. I never did. I respected my parents. I didn't particularly like my siblings.

"With Lily, it was the reverse. As I had too little, she had too much. The relatives who brought her up reminded her of that daily. It was her duty to give, to share with the less fortunate; but she must be careful not to foster intimacy. Most people — men and women, boys and girls — would be interested only in the money. I wasn't. I could swear that on whatever I hold most sacred, and people of course wouldn't believe me. Lily did. She recognized a need in me just as I recognized a need in her. We were perfectly aware of the rumor, gossip, even malice — a young man, an older woman; a very poor young man, a very rich older woman. Neither of us blamed anyone."

Maggie said, "Please sit down. . . . Katie's always telling Jeremy that he 'looms.' You do too."

"I'm sorry. As I said last night, recently I've often had too much to drink. I could use that excuse, it wouldn't have been true."

Maggie said, after a moment, pushing her mop of red curls from her forehead and looking at him with candid blue eyes, "I still don't see why me — unless it was merely because I'm female."

"No . . . well . . . somewhat, perhaps, but certainly not altogether. I like you, Maggie, we all do — "

He was including Kim, but she asked, "Lily?"

"Yes. More than the other young women

— oh, she likes them well enough, but she enjoys being with you — or did. She told me once, 'I could have had a daughter her age.' ''

''Perhaps if you talked to Ben — '' Maggie began.

''Ben's a fine man, and a good physician — but no. I don't think I can talk to anyone about Lily except you. I was astonished last night to find that I could and you're a great deal younger than I.'' he added.

She said, ''I've always liked what's known as 'older men,' probably because I didn't know my father, and because I love my stepfather very much. But I've been afraid of you,'' she ended.

''Afraid?'' His eyebrows rose. He could not credit his hearing. This young woman — well balanced, vibrant and in her own fashion very attractive. . . . ''Why?''

For some inexplicable reason she was now, for the first time in her knowledge of him, uninhibited and at ease. She said cheerfully, ''I was afraid of falling in love with you. I suppose a lot of women have been.''

''Oh?'' he said gravely. ''The image? I

once thought why slave, why kill yourself trying to be a doctor? Even if you get through, how can you equip an office? You'll be in debt for the rest of your life. So I considered Hollywood and television. Perhaps after all I had something to sell. I had no control over the way my face was put together; my mother was beautiful — too fat but beautiful; she aged soon, of course. My father was, I suppose, average in appearance. I had one really beautiful sister — the easiest way for her was to become a tramp — quite early. She prospered until she died."

"Alan — I didn't mean — "

"Forget it. Yes, certainly women have thought themselves in love with me — girls, older women. Some offered me money," he said, "but I was selective. Before I knew Lily, the only women I was intimate with neither charged *nor* paid; and when they exhibited possessiveness, I walked out."

"What happened to Hollywood?" Maggie asked after a moment.

"I was in my last year of medical school — we were allowed to work in the wards under supervision — when I met a man — a patient, not in a ward but a private room — who had what's known as connections. When he painted a pretty fantastic picture of what I might expect, I accepted an introduction and a loan and flew out to the Coast. He had a big investment in one of the studios. The way was smoothed for me. I was greeted amiably, photographed from all angles and given a screen test, which I failed, but I remember the girl who played the little scene with me; she's done very well, I see her on television. That was, of course, before they required you to remove your clothes," he added. "Anyway I flew home, began my internship and, over a period of time, I finally repaid my benefactor. Incidentally he let me live in his well-stocked apartment the short time I was on the Coast. It was also well staffed, which terrified me."

"Have you seen him since?"

"Oh yes — he's been in the hospital several times. I even had an opportunity to test him for allergies a year or so before we came here."

"Why *did* you come here?" she asked.

"We were tired of having people gossip about us although our story, I believe, has followed us to Little Oxford. Also, Lily thought Kim was less likely to hear discussion in school here away from where he and his mother were born."

Maggie said, "Kim would have clobbered any kid who put you or Lily down."

He laughed; and then stopped. "That's the first time I've laughed in a long time," he said, "and I was laughing about something which has to do with Kim. . . . Thank you, Maggie. Well, it's getting late. I'm sorry — must be close to your suppertime. I'd suggest that you come out with me, but it probably wouldn't suit you or be very sensible."

She said, "Even if Lily won't go out, you should — with lots of people."

"I doubt that she'd even notice," he said somberly. "If I said, 'I'm going out and getting drunk,' she'd probably answer, 'I don't think it would be wise, but if that's what you want . . .' You see, in effect, she's always said 'if that's what you want' during all the twelve years of our marriage."

Maggie went to the door with him. It was still and warm, the shadows long and gold, and tonight there would be a new moon.

"Maggie, please come and see Lily again."

"She doesn't want to see me, or anybody, Alan."

"I know, but please? It frightens me to have her so alone. People are kind; they come often; they coax her to do things, and she does, when it's for a charity or of course for the Foundation."

"I'll try. . . . My sister's coming to visit me next month. Perhaps Lily would let me bring her — "

"I'm sure she would. She loved Hawaii," he said. "We went to all the islands — that first time." He fell silent. "May I come back and just talk?" he asked.

"If you wish," she said, no longer plagued by something which might have been guilt, because for the first time she not only felt at ease but saw him not as an image, not as a projection of her silver-screen fantasies, but as he was, an unhappy, tormented man with no strength in him.

Now the dogwood creamed rosily over, and the apple trees bloomed — all the springtime marvels. It was Maggie's first spring in the north and Matt, taking her to dinner at the Greek restaurant where everyone knew him, said, "Eat, drink, and dance the whatever it's called. This is Lee's favorite haunt, and Stacy's too. I meant to bring you before, but then it's prettier at this time. Have you anything like this in Hawaii? Spring, I mean."

She said reproachfully, "Ours is practically year round."

"I should never have asked. When's Lani due?"

"Last I heard, mid-June. I don't know her flight yet. If it's a Saturday or Sunday, I'll drive into town and meet her. Otherwise, she can take the limousine."

"No one, least of all Aunt Hattie, would trust you driving into the city. She probably screams at the nearest cloud every time she looks down at her car."

"Don't be silly," Maggie said. "I take very good care of it — spit and polish, lots of washings, proper oil changes."

"And scratches?"

"Everyone gets scratched or dented; it's become a way of life. And the car still runs. It had better because I certainly can't afford a new one."

When they were having coffee, he said casually, "Aunt Hattie wouldn't like your seeing St. Luke the Less as much as you do. I spot his car at her door often."

"There isn't a St. Luke the Less, only a St. James. I never quite knew why he was the Less. . . . You mean Alan Carstairs, of course. I'm sure Aunt Hattie wouldn't mind."

"Give me one good reason."

"I can give you several. He's not interested in me and I'm not in love with him. Like every other female in this benighted village, I was sure I could be or even was, a little, if from a distance. Not now. No way. He comes to see me so he has someone to talk to — not *with,* I guess, just *at.* I like him, I like Lily, and I'm scared."

"Why?"

She said soberly, "I can't tell you, Matt. All I can say is he's in exile and it's destroying him."

"Well . . ." said Matt, and, after a moment, "I believe you. I haven't the least idea why. Where's my logic? Look at the circumstantial evidence! Can anyone help? No one knows him well, I guess, except now, possibly, you."

"That's only recently. I suggested talking with Ben — he wouldn't."

Matt said, frowning, "But isn't it usual? I mean, Kim was their only child, born later in Lily's life than is usual for a first. Is it so surprising she's shut herself away from everyone — including her husband — which is, I imagine, what you mean."

"Of course not. But if it goes on — I mean — there's danger isn't there, for her?"

"I would think so, but I'm not qualified to answer. Dad had a client once who withdrew from the world about him — very gradually. No one realized it — not his wife or his children — until it was too late. Then even the psychiatrist couldn't help. . . . Don't look so parental, Magpie."

"Parental?"

"Oh, mothering, soothing. I don't know

if it's me you're mothering or Alan."

"Not you," she said. "No one ever needed assistance less. . . . How's your love life? I haven't kept up."

"Boring. Do you think Lani would like me to fall ravenously in love with her?"

"She'd be pleased, but she's used to it, Matt, so it would come as no surprise."

"It would to me," he said, "and she can't be half as devastating as you've often suggested."

But all Maggie said was, "Wait and see. She's some *wahini,* which means woman."

"Thanks for the translation and, incidentally, St. James the Less was merely shorter than St. James the Great."

"How do you know?"

"When I was seventeen," he answered gravely, "I attended an adult Sunday-school class. I also dated the teacher."

"You're impossible."

"Merely improbable. Let's go, shall we? We can walk around for the good of our digestion; actually we should jog home."

When he left her, he said, "Remember, when you learn when Lani's coming, let me know. Perhaps I can arrange to meet her."

"I've asked her to come on a Saturday or Sunday. I hope she will. Thanks just the same."

"Oh, in that case I'll drive you. I wouldn't feel comfortable otherwise. Aunt Hattie would expect it of me. I am not criticizing your driving — it saw you through a northern winter — but the way to the airport is long, hard and strewn with good and bad intentions. My father wouldn't forgive me either; he doesn't like to lose a client."

He bent his head and kissed her cheek. "And I do relish," he added, "a platonic relationship as it's so rare."

12

Vanessa Steele bicycled over the back roads and straighter streets in the May afternoon. Shadow sat in his basket, his leash coiled beside him, and muttered. There were too many cars, also people. He remembered when things had been quieter, but they'd changed since his ignorant kittenhood. On the whole he preferred his own place. The woman in his life had also changed, he further reflected, and wondered why. It is not given to people with four feet to recognize age in bipeds.

Vanessa was also reflecting. Not since Stacy's arrival in Little Oxford had she taken to a young person as she had to Maggie Knox.

"I don't understand her," she told herself. "I could Stacy — unhappy, talented, even neurotic — I could relate to her, but this youngster, too honest, too —

well, even wholesome" — she shuddered slightly — "to be real, like her grandaunt. And she is real. I suppose I'm cracking up and at an age when anything young appeals, birds, kittens puppies. . . . "

She parked her vehicle at the side, went around front and up Maggie's steps with Shadow sulking on his leash.

Maggie opened the door. "Come in," she said. "I was watching for you."

"Mind if Shadow cases the joint?" Vanessa asked. "He's been housebroken for almost as long as he's lived and only knocks things over when angry. He's annoyed at me now, but he won't destroy anything of yours. He just hates being leashed."

"Please let him off," Maggie said.

Vanessa released the catch and Shadow preceded them, without haste, into the living room. Vanessa looked around her. "Nice. Good vibrations, which is naturally to be expected. Was it like this when you came?"

"Oh, yes. I've added very little, and taken away nothing except the footstool Andrew Comstock liked and the watercolor Aunt Hattie left to Matt."

"I understood she left him some money too."

"Honestly, Mrs. Steele!" Maggie exclaimed, exasperated.

"Call me Van, it's easier. . . . Where do I get my information?" She laughed and pushed her hand through her unruly hair. "People of course, all sorts of perople. . . . Everyone knows everything in this area — or thinks he does. I believe it was our mutual friend and helper, Mrs. Green, who said the money was really for the dog. I appreciate that," she added, "even though her taste in animals left something to be desired."

Maggie laughed. She said, "I can't be annoyed with you — that is for long. Yes, Aunt Hattie knew how he felt about Moxie; the money was for delicacies. Moxie has costly gourmet preferences."

Vanessa looked at Shadow prowling around, sniffing, drawing back in distaste. "There's something here he doesn't trust," she said, sitting down.

Maggie's eyes followed her guest's. "Oh!" she said. "Matt sits over there often. Moxie usually lies beside him."

"That accounts for it. Stop prowling, you aren't in the jungle — which isn't quite accurate," she added, "when you consider the world as it has become. Find a place. Sit or lie in it, go to sleep. Maggie will give you your tea with a little jolt of something," she advised, "not sugar and milk. . . . I'll help."

"No," said Maggie. "Everything's ready," and as Vanessa inexorably followed her into the kitchen, "What will you have in yours? I have rum and a little brandy."

"Rum," said Vanessa, "and for Shadow. We are probably too old — he in his way, I in mine — to become alcoholics. But at our age a slight stimulant is good for the arteries, so we indulge — at tea time and with supper, a small amount of wine. . . . You've changed the kitchen?"

"Not really. Just added a few gadgets to make things simpler, being a working woman."

"You like the hospital?"

"Very much, especially on days off, like this. Seriously, I enjoy the work. I was trained for it, you know."

"I understand you've done some work for Dr. Carstairs after hours," Vanessa observed.

"Typing," Maggie said briefly, and took the tray into the living room. Her hands didn't shake, but she was shaken.

Vanessa, offering Shadow his tea and rum in a saucer, said, "Don't be upset, Maggie."

"I'm not," Maggie denied furiously.

"Pour the tea," Vanessa suggested, and when tea and cookies had been courteously offered she said, "Care to tell me about it?"

Maggie was wide-eyed with disbelief. *"You?"* she asked.

"Yes. One thing you've yet to learn. When I ask impertinent questions and repeat the answers, the information has come from someone else."

"Unimpeachable sources?"

"Is there such a word as 'peachable'?" Vanessa inquired. "No one is unimpeachable. It's all colored by the minds through which the information passes. You soon learn to recognize that,

Maggie. But when the person involved trusts me — and as has often happened, confides in me — nothing is ever repeated."

Maggie believed her, but didn't understand why. She said, "Somehow I believe that, Van."

"Of course I ask questions in order to learn and to satisfy my insatiable curiosity — just so. Were you a Kipling reader as a child? And then when someone asks, I make an effort to help. I can't always, of course, But it seems to me that I've lived long and hard enough to have experienced almost every situation and temptation, of course from my personal angle. . . . Are you in love with Carstairs?"

"No."

Vanessa looked at her. She asked, "Sure of that?"

"I wasn't for a while."

"He's a beautiful man, physically," Vanessa said, "but a Greek god is beautiful in his fashion. So are a lot of carved or painted men. But what ticks? I wonder what animates him. Who is he? I haven't the least idea."

Maggie said, "A man with a tragedy."

"Few of us live without tragedy," Vanessa said. "Stacy has told me Lily Carstairs sees very few people. This is comprehensible to me. I don't know her very well, but I judge her to be deeply emotional and also exclusive."

Maggie said after a moment, "Alan's been to see me a few times, Van. We've had lunch maybe twice at the hospital. I'm just so sorry for him."

"Naturally," Vanessa said, "but that's dangerous, after a while. And men don't really want pity. Compassion yes, we all need that; pity, no." She added casually, "However, I don't think Alan Carstairs is a strong man, and I don't mean physically."

Startled, Maggie asked, "What makes you say that?"

"His wife," Vanessa told her, "is an unusually strong woman. . . . You don't think so? You think if she were strong she would have emerged from the darkness of the child's death? With the chin-up attitude? Oh, no. . . . I know a little about her, from others of course, and I've met her as you know. She's not given to the stiff

198

upper lip. Her strength is inner and simply exists. It hasn't hardened her emotions. She's not going to put on a mask — or pretend something she doesn't feel. I was once, " said Vanessa, "very like her. . . . May I have some tea?"

Maggie poured, and as Vanessa took up the little silver pitcher with rum in it, Shadow came across the room.

"You've had enough," Vanessa said. "Remember your liver."

In reply, with a sidelong glance, he leaped into his startled hostess's lap and remained there, purring.

"Doesn't do that often, except to Stacy. Once upon a time he practically lived in a beautiful Chinese bowl on her mantel. I am not jealous, however. He's punishing me," Vanessa said with her wide infectious smile. "But I believe he likes you. . . . Where were we?"

"You said you were rather like Lily."

"Only in the strength and the inability to mask anything. I was also once very like you, and ," she added with vigor, "a hell of a lot of other idiotic women."

"In what way?"

"Being sorry; letting down the guard. Forget it," Vanessa advised her. "You aren't helping; nothing you can do would. Grief's grief and it manifests in various ways and depths — it's like love — you can't reproach the saucer for not holding as much as the cup or the cup for not being as full as the pitcher. Men have various ways of trying to console themselves — drink, women, work. I daresay if you offered to go to bed with him, he'd accept. But it wouldn't do any good," she added. "I think it's his wife he wants and can't have, at least now."

Maggie asked, after a moment, "What makes you think that?"

"No one's suggested it to me if that's what you mean," Vanessa said. "It's simply that I've met women like Lily before, also men like her husband. No one is wholly unique except, of course, to himself." She rose and Shadow slid from Maggie's lap. "We'll go along now," she said briskly. "If you ask us, we'll come back. You come see us and bring your stepsister, and I didn't get that from distant sources — just Stacy."

"Stacy's been wonderful," Maggie said, going with them to the door. "Amy too — everyone. I'll be working while Lani's here; they've promised to look after her."

They stood together a moment. The bright sky was starting to fade and Vanessa said, "People talk about the sunset of life." She laughed. "It isn't really. Old age is what it's made of itself. Sun, rain, light, darkness. At my age you think a good deal about dying — not death, really, just dying. And it frightens you, when you wake in the night and find you're amazed that you *do* wake. My son irritates me; my grandson, my friends, my doctors. I mustn't live alone, they say; but I wouldn't live with my son and his wife for all the oil in Arabia. I'm too healthy for a nursing home, and a so-called retirement home — my son has even offered to buy a place for me as my principal is in trust for Adam, my grandson — means a large pleasant room, good meals, companions my own age and the watchful eyes of the trained young. I can't imagine anything more difficult for me to adapt to. Every night I say my prayers — ask Stacy, she knows — and I ask for the same thing. A rousing good heart failure, arrest, or whatever they call it — a coronary? — in my sleep. Shadow's provided for. Stacy and Lee will take him." She put her lean, cool hand on Maggie's cheek. "You're a nice girl," she said. "Don't waste your time. You've a lot of it, but, still, don't waste it. Keep some in the bank, at interest. 'Bye."

Down the steps she went with Shadow after her, and then wheeling into the beginning dusk. Maggie stood there looking after them. She thought: I'm beginning to understand why Lee and Stacy and Drs. Bing and Ben are so fond of her. Yet, she's an eccentric, egotistical, prying, interfering old woman. Lani would believe in the witch theory; anyone born in the Islands believes in a lot of inexplicable intangibles. I do too. Even if I wasn't born in the Islands, I've lived there most of my life. "Anyway, I like her," Maggie said to the evening star.

It was growing late. She had the tea things to wash and she had to get dressed. She was going to the Inn with the

Comstock men and she'd better be ready; it was a Saturday night.

She was on the steps when Alan's car stopped and he got out and came toward her. He said, "Could I persuade you to give me a drink before I go — " he paused, "home?"

"I'm sorry," Maggie told him. "I have a dinner date and I'll just about make it. Vanessa Steele was here for tea and I couldn't abide leaving dirty dishes."

"That's all right," he said, and went back to his car.

She thought: Perhaps I should. . . . No. She squared her shoulders. Vanessa was right. I can solve nothing.

It occurred to her that perhaps at the beginning she hadn't really wanted to solve anything and a hot impatience invaded her . . . with Alan, and yes, with Lily.

At dinner, Maggie announced with conscious pride, "Vanessa Steele and Shadow had tea with me."

Matt eyed her with respect and his father said, "I've tried often to get her to visit us and succeeded only once — no twice. But of course she wouldn't bring

Shadow — because of Moxie."

Moxie was with them tonight, out by the small switchboard, lying beside the pretty blonde operator, looking smug. Later he'd be invited into the coat room — where there were no coats — and offered a slight, but commendable, tidbit.

"Actually she could have," said Matt. "Moxie has met Vanessa's familiar several times, and always behaved like a perfect German aristocrat."

Andrew asked, as the drinks came, "You've seen her often, Maggie?"

"Oh, at that Christmas party — and Stacy took me to her house — absolutely fantastic, all those things — and she was at Ben's and Amy's . . . anyway she consented to come to tea. I felt as if I'd been asked to entertain royalty, and I have no idea why."

"She's rare. Ben would explain that she's like a very rare book. Scarcity is its real value — not just age."

"I know Stacy worries about her and I think I found out why."

"Oh, the hopefully impending heart attack?" Andrew said and studied the menu. "What are you two having?"

They ordered and then Maggie asked, "You know about it?"

"That she prays for a quick departure from her own bed? Of course. I'm her lawyer. I've talked to Bing and also to Ben. For her age, it's a sound heart. But I understand her dread of a long mentally or physically crippling illness."

After a moment, Maggie said, "I hope her prayers are answered."

"Well," said Andrew, "she did tell me that she didn't think she'd earned it."

"She asked me to bring Lani to see her. . . . Incidentally, Matt, Lani will be in Georgia for that wedding next week. The wedding's Saturday, and she'll stay over and arrive here midweek. Apparently a weekend didn't suit her."

Matt said soothingly, "Don't fret. I'll look at my calendar. I don't think I've too much on after this week, for a while; some closings as I recall it, and a divorce case" — he made a crinkled face at his father. "You were so right to let me handle it," he said. "experience is the best teacher. And a woman in hysterics and the screaming meemies even better."

Maggie said doubtfully, "I was going to ask for the day off."

"What time does she get in?"

"Late afternoon."

"Good, ask for an hour. I'll drive. My car. We'll take her to dinner, but only," he added, "because I'm anxious to meet and overwhelm her."

"Sorry about that," said Maggie.

13

"We will meet you," Maggie informed Lani by phone, "at the baggage counter."

"Who's we?" Lani asked, from Atlanta.

"Matt Comstock. He's offered to drive and also take us to dinner."

"Sounds promising. Matt, as I remember, is the lawyer who isn't good-looking; attractive, though not your type."

"Greg told me to work on you. He wants you back with us. I do too, but I felt I must warn you. I am, after all, almost irresistible and you should be given a fair chance."

"So, I'm warned. 'Bye, dear. See you Wednesday."

On Wednesday, shortly before six, Maggie and Matt were waiting. The plane was on time, but, as Matt remarked, getting from it to luggage was another matter — or else you got there ahead of your luggage and waited.

"Maggie, you're dancing around like a kid in a playground. People will think you're my little daughter, particularly if I seize your arm in a brutal grip, which I'll do in a moment." He looked at the big clock on the wall and at his watch. "She ought to be along soon."

"Where are we going for dinner? I forgot to ask you."

"How about Polynesian Paradise?"

"Matt, no, for heaven's sake, not Lani. For me, yes, it would be fun by now."

"Well, seeing she's been south," Matt said, "she may have eaten her weight in fried chicken, hominy grits, turnip greens and pecan pie — "

"Sounds marvelous."

"Anything does, as far as you're concerned. You eat more than any girl I've ever known. . . . There's a sort of pub-type place situated in a big apartment-house complex, with parking too. Quite spectacular, people drift in now and then, like us. Also, TV and radio slaves and reporters. Hey — "

But Maggie was off and running. Lani

had arrived and, as she was taller than Maggie, Matt managed his first glimpse of her. "Holy mackerel!" he said reverently.

Still waiting for the luggage, he looked again as they approached, and noted that the young women were paying no attention to him or his patient vigil. After a moment he said gravely, "Miss Knox?"

"Lani — Iolani to be exact," she said and they moved to the counter.

"Lani. . . . You've had a very good press in the person of our Maggie."

"H. Margaret," Maggie corrected him. "Haven't you ever looked at my legal signature? Or seen checks? Your father knows."

"What does the H stand for?" Matt asked, stunned.

"Harriet, of course. I can't imagine what else you'd think."

"Hortense. Hell. Heloise. Hupmobile."

"Don't go on. Mother named me for Aunt Harriet, who hated her own name. Hence, a compromise."

"Give over," Lani said imperiously. "Here come my bits and pieces."

Eventually, with the aid of a porter and a

cart, they were out of the airport and Matt had found his car miraculously nearby.

"Whom did you bribe?" asked Maggie suspiciously.

"No one. I simply paid an amiable young man to drive around and around until he found a place fairly close to the exit doors."

At a table in the low-ceilinged, timbered restaurant, complete with bar, dart board and a great gathering of bottles inserted into the walls, Matt said, after the drinks had been ordered, "You more than live up to your press, Lani."

Long, heavy, straight-falling black hair, incredibly blue-gray eyes and a flawless skin, tanned, but not as deeply as Maggie's had been. No freckles. And walking behind her into the restaurant, it had not escaped Matt's notice that she was marvelously shaped.

"Maggie's prejudiced," she said, "but, thanks."

Maggie, studying the menu, asked, "Can you afford steaks?"

Matt answered, "Just on special

occasions, of which this is indubitably one.''

''Very pricey,'' agreed Lani. ''But then so's Honolulu.''

''How come the slight British overlay?'' Matt inquired.

''Well,'' said Maggie, before Lani could answer, ''Lani plays the international field. I understand there's an Australian and I believe there's a delightful young man at the British consulate — ''

''I also know some New Zealanders,'' said Lani. ''South Africans and Canadians. You name it. Everyone comes to the Islands sooner or later.''

''I must remember that,'' said Matt. He raised his glass. ''Cheers or whatever's appropriate. Since Maggie's a working girl, Lani, I'll see you around in my lighter moments, so you won't lack for entertainment.''

''I've a schedule all ready for her,'' Maggie said. ''Dinners — well I'm included — lunches, shopping trips — ''

''Including one to the Capitol with me, I hope,'' Matt said. ''Monday and early.'' He gave their order, and until it came, listened. "Feel free," he'd said, "to talk as if I weren't here." Therefore he heard some of Maggie's impressions of New England and their cozy village, while Lani responded with hometown news — weddings, divorces, affairs, funerals and scandals.

"We must bore you," Lani told Matt, smiling. She had the most beautiful teeth he'd ever seen; also hands.

"I'm never bored. It all adds up to experience, as I look for flaws, so to speak, in the evidence, or methinks sometimes the witness doth protest too much — that sort of thing."

"Suspicious by nature," Maggie said. "Lani, did you bring a guitar?"

"For heaven's sake, no! Did you expect I'd perform at Carolyn's wedding?"

"Of course not. Well, I have mine. Vi sent it on, and with any luck it won't be too late when we get home."

"No concert tonight," Lani said firmly. "I want to look around, unpack, go to bed and sleep until noon."

"You shall. I'll give you my alarm clock."

When they reached Little Oxford, Matt had amassed considerable information. The use of an occasional Hawaiian word didn't dismay him. Maggie usually translated — but it was evident that the words and usage were as common to both of them as English.

The highway wasn't crowded and they reached Little Oxford in excellent time. Mrs. Green had been by to put on lights, draw curtains, and set out coffee things for later, or breakfast. And Lani cried going in, "I love it!"

"Where's she sleeping?" asked Matt, his hands full of luggage.

"Aunt Hattie's room."

"So you never moved in after all?"

"No, I like it where I am. So Aunt Hattie's room is the guest room."

"Since when am I a guest?" Lani inquired.

"I don't mean that exactly. I know it's my house and you're my sister, but I still feel a little like a guest myself; a beloved guest," Maggie added stoutly. "Anyway, you liked Aunt Hattie, and she loved you, so she'll be glad you're here."

"Don't worry about her," Lani told Matt as they started upstairs. "She's always been that way. We all are, a little, in the Islands. . . . What a delightful room, and how like her!"

"Exactly," said Maggie, "and as Van would say, good vibrations."

"Who's Van?"

"Our local witch," Matt said. "You must meet her. You probably once belonged to the same coven, all three of you."

"Don't be facetious," Maggie said. "Lani's heard the army marching; she's heard the drums."

"I hope she won't hear them here," said Matt with resignation.

"You two go back downstairs," said Lani in a slightly regal way. "I want to unpack a couple of gifts. I've one for you, Matt."

"How come?"

"I knew you'd be around."

Once downstairs, Matt asked Maggie, "What did you tell her?"

"Very little, just originally, I said you were your father's son."

"Nice of you to concede that."

"And attractive," she added. "What do you think of her?"

"Come to think of it, I don't know. I like her, who wouldn't? She's beautiful and, I assume, intelligent. She's also a menace to almost every other woman. She and Alan Carstairs would be a marvelous pair."

"Really, Matt!"

"Don't be indignant. I'm sure Aunt Hattie would say, 'Handsome is as handsome does.' "

"She never said anything like that in her life."

"But think how they'd look together; the antithesis of Grant Wood's couple. But that wouldn't be practical. Which one would hog the mirror?"

"Lani isn't vain!"

"Don't clench your fists at me. Maybe not. Oddly enough I don't think Carstairs is either."

"What are you quarreling about?" Lani inquired. Her footfall was muted. She walked as lightly as a feather blows.

"You are really a creep," Matt said comfortably. "Sit down. Your sister has no manners. Put your feet up. We were talking about a spectacular-looking mutual friend, a male. I suggested you'd make a striking couple, but that one of you might sulk."

Lani put her feet up as directed and laughed. She said, "Maggie knows I'm not vain. Why should I be? I'm as God and my genes created me. I see myself every day and I'm pleased that I needn't worry about my appearance. It saves a lot of time and trouble. But I've never figured out why anyone would be vain because of something they can't really *help* — looks, brains, talents. . . . Of course you can improve on what's given you."

"What's in the packages?" Maggie asked.

"Catch. It won't break, I hope. That's yours. I brought Matt a Tiki."

"What's that?" Matt asked cautiously as she gave him a small tissue-wrapped object. He opened it, disclosing a singularly ugly little carving in greenstone.

"New Zealand. A Maori god. The good ones, of course, are in museums or private collections — very old and of different sizes. This is, I suppose, machine made for tourist trade. But they're lucky. Also, as a warning, I must tell you I think he's the god of fertility," Lani said.

Matt, dropping and hastily retrieving the Tiki, asked, "A male god?"

"Yes. Does it matter in the new dawn of unisex? Carry him in your pocket. He'll win you a lot of cases — I don't know of what. . . . You like your bottle, Maggie?"

"Love it. I had one before I left home, remember. I think Vi used up all the perfume and I gave her the bottle to keep."

A heavy perfume, in a slender glass tube inside a wooden bottle. "Good God," said Matt, rearing back as Maggie opened it and held it under his nose.

"She'll use only half a drop," Lani reassured him. "Look at the bottle; it's monkey pod."

"What are the stones?"

"Olivines," said Lani.

A car came by, slowed down, backed up, and stopped.

"Expecting anyone?" Matt asked.

"No," Maggie said.

Someone came up the steps and Maggie went to the door. "Well, hi," she said.

Alan Carstairs, following her as she returned to the room, saw Matt and a girl in a bright-flowered housecoat — only it wasn't a housecoat.

"I'm Lani of the Islands," the girl said, smiling.

"Dr. Carstairs," Maggie told her sister.

And Lani said, with a sidelong glance at Matt, "I should have known him anywhere."

"I saw your car," Alan told Matt. "I'd always recognize it."

"Best beat-up expensive heap in town," Matt agreed.

"Do sit down, Alan," Maggie urged him.

"Thanks, I just wanted to be sure you were in. I'll be back in a minute." He went out and they heard him running down the steps.

"How about it?" said Matt. "Now you've met our local Apollo, Aphrodite."

Alan came back, a box of flowers in his arm. "For you," he told Lani, "from my wife. She believes everyone prefers to arrange their own."

"Into the kitchen," Maggie ordered, seizing the box, and they trooped after her. All the spring blooms. Tulips, marigolds, jonquils.

"Lilacs," said Alan sadly, "are gone, and I wish you'd been here for the dogwood."

"I'll put these in pitchers," Maggie said. "Lani can fix them later. Let's go back to the living room."

But Alan had to leave. He said, giving Lani a small envelope, "From my wife, a welcome."

He went to the door, raised his hand, and smiled. "Good night," he said.

"How nice of her!" Lani said, reading the note. "She wants me to come — with you, of course, Maggie — for luncheon on Saturday."

After a moment, Matt said, "She's trying."

"Trying what?" Lani asked.

"To live I guess," Matt answered. "You tell her, Maggie."

Lani's eyes were soft and bright. She said, "Now I remember. The people you wrote me about — the little boy. Oh," she added simply, "the poor things! ... I wonder if we should go. It must be an effort for her."

"It's an effort she should make for her own sake," Matt said. "You go on to bed now, Lani. I'll see you soon. Get some rest. You too, Maggie. Remember, you have work to do and I don't expect you to neglect it except when I'm campaigning. Lock up after me, girls."

They locked up; Lani arranged the flowers in various appropriate containers, and went upstairs.

Maggie made coffee and brought it up to her sister, who was brushing her hair by the dressing table. "You always liked it at bedtime," she said.

"Only if we were sitting up all night, which we aren't tonight," Lani said yawning. "I've so much to tell you — about the wedding and — "

"Any proposals?"

"At the wedding? Oh yes, three; one man was married, one was drunk. Par for the course. It will all keep."

"Serious about your Australian?"

"Not really. . . . Here, let me look at

your room again, and the study. Really, it's a delightful house. I may not be able to pry you out of it."

"What do you think of Matt?"

"Just what you do — not good-looking, very attractive and not my type. Although as to that," Lani added frankly, "I don't know many who really aren't — it's just that I don't think he digs me . . . which, come to think of it, should make him wildly interesting."

"Here's a radio clock," Maggie said. "Set it for anytime between eleven and twelve. I'll leave the makings of breakfast — fruit juice, the coffee measured. Amy Irvington will come by for you at quarter to one." She kissed her sister. "I'm so glad you're here," she said.

She went to bed and cried a little, because she was both happy and homesick.

14

Everyone in Mr. Davis's office, the
volunteers in the coffee shop and anyone
else who had heard of Maggie's impending,
and now resident, houseguest was happy
for her. . . .

"She rollicks," Mrs. Cromwell told Mr.
Davis, "of course in a quiet way."

"What an extraordinary verb!" he
comented.

"I know. I've never used it before." She
pushed a pencil through her neat white
coiffure. "But it somehow suits her."

Maggie knocked, came in smiling and
Mrs. Cromwell admitted that she had just
been talking about her. "I told the boss you
rollicked," she said.

"Sounds noisy," Maggie complained.

"Well, you're not. Do bring your sister
to see us and the hospital."

"I'll try. Unlike me, she hates hospitals.

Not that she's ever had anything worse than childhood ailments and an occasional cold — but I remember when Greg was in the hospital with pneumonia it was all I could do to drag her there. . . . He's her father," she explained.

They knew, they said

When Maggie reached home, opened the door and looked, it was empty downstairs, but faint sounds reached her from above.

She ran upstairs to find Lani stretched on the couch in the study, a glass of iced tea beside her and the television on.

"At this time of day?" asked Maggie.

"Don't you, ever?"

"Oh, football, sports, whatever — a Saturday or Sunday sometimes. Do turn it off."

"Just when our heroine was nerving herself to tell all," said Lani mournfully. "I didn't hear you come in."

"I sneaked in. I'm a big girl now. I have a key."

"I meant, the car."

"Gosh," Maggie said, and cast her linen jacket aside, "it's so damned hot. Not fair, in June." She looked with envy at Lani in her voluminous bright garment. "I could kill you," she said. "Nothing has ever been invented as cool and comfortable as the Polynesian Mother Hubbard."

"You had dozens."

"Some wore out in California, and when I decided to stay here, I wrote Vi she could have what I'd left in the apartment. She's about my size. Honestly, Lani, it never occurred to me it would be so hot here — and they tell me it can be during any month from May to October."

"Amy brought me home an hour and a half ago," Lani said. "I like her. I asked her to come in, but she had to get back to the nursery. I think she believes the baby-sitter puts spells on that child. He's delicious. I could eat him with a spoon. When I marry, I plan to have four, with, of course, cooperation and consent."

"Won't you have trouble getting the Flying Doctors to the Outback?" asked Maggie. "Is that all the tea you made?"

"No. There's a pitcher, and a glass over on the small table."

"I'll never live through the summer,"

Maggie predicted. "Of course the offices and some other parts of the hospital are air-conditioned and they're getting around to the patients' rooms gradually. But when you come out on a day like this, hit the outside air and then the parking lot, it's murder. They say it usually cools off at night."

"I don't know why you're complaining," Lani said. "Southern California isn't exactly Alaska. And haven't you noticed our own Kona weather in September and October?"

"I'd forgotten. I guess when you leave home, you remember only the wonderful things. . . . Where'd you have lunch?"

"At Amy's. I suppose she took one look at me — I was wearing this rag — and decided to eat in."

"No. You could turn up in a bikini and she'd take you wherever she'd planned. She'd stand her ground and fight for your rights even if she disapproved of your costume. That's Voltaire — I think. I'll ask Jeremy."

"Who's he? Jeremy, I mean — I know who Voltaire was."

"Local bookseller, collector, charmer and co-author of the book I sent Greg. You'll meet him and his wife."

"Good. They all have wives here, don't they? Amy's husband came in for about six minutes as we were having lunch. He's quite a guy. Worth falling ill for, but I always look so dreadful when I do. He liked the Mother Hubbard. I said it was a mumu, which I think he connects with a cow. I told Amy I'd send her one; I'll send you several. Bit by bit we'll invade Little Oxford. . . . Dr. Carstairs — I wonder how his patients react. What is he, a surgeon?"

"No, he specializes in dermatology and allergies."

"Skin troubles I don't have; allergies I could. Maggie, I've been prowling around — it's compulsory, my feline instinct — so I know where everything is. I'll set the table. How many are we?"

"Just us tonight. Tomorrow, Matt's house. You'll love his father. Saturday, of course, the Carstairs' for lunch."

"Will he be there?"

"I expect so."

"What's she like?"

"Lovely."

"What kind of lovely?" Lani asked.

"Inside. Outside, plain except for the eyes," Maggie explained briefly. They had spoken for years in a sort of shorthand.

"I'm going to take a shower," Maggie announced, "then we'll fix supper."

When she surfaced, she wore the most comfortable frock she owned — A-line, sleeveless, short and loose. Lani was downstairs setting the table. "Not that I know what we're eating," she remarked.

"Sour — cold — an enormous salad, and the wine Matt selected is on ice."

It was growing dark when they sat down in the dining room. "Kitchen's too hot," said Maggie. "There's lawn furniture outside. Aunt Hattie's. I put it out a week ago. I think when I can afford it, I'll have a little patio built near the back door and buy a glass and iron table and chairs."

"You sound as if you really mean to stay here."

"I do. I've told you that."

"What's the attraction, Maggie?"

"Well, I like it. I like the village, the

house, the people. I lived through a winter and it didn't kill me.''

''Must be more than that. There's always a serious reason for decisions.''

''My mother was born and grew up here, Lani.''

''I know. But when you left home for California, Maggie, it was the silliest thing you ever did.''

Maggie said shortly, ''I'll get the salad.''

She removed the thin soup bowls and brought in the salad — lettuce, vegetables, scallions from a farm near Vanessa's, anchovies, sardines, capers, celery from the supermarket, crab and lobster meat from the fishman, and her own excellent dressing.

''You name it,'' said Lani appreciatively, ''it's all in here. I'm glad you like to cook.''

''You still don't?''

''I dislike the idea intensely. But I love to plan meals and give orders, which is what I do a good many times a week.''

''What's Greg doing without you?''

''Kazui functions, just as she always has. After all, she's been with us since mother died. And there won't be any real company — just Denis perhaps, and a few insiders. Dad's away a lot — mostly the other islands on business, and to look at the Big Island property. . . . I've never seen plates like these, Maggie.''

"Aunt Hattie's. The Chinese bowls are too; the ironstone chowder plates are great for chowder, stew, pasta, almost anything, but a little deep for salad. . . . How's the wine?''

"Light, good and cold. It will probably make us hotter than ever, but it creates the illusion of coolness first. Buy some rum and I'll make planter's punch before I leave." She raised her glass. "Here's to your homecoming," she said.

"Oh, hush," Maggie said. "Now I'm certain you're going to Australia and want me to return and father-sit.''

"I'm not going anywhere. I've no such intention and never have. You know Greg's going to retire eventually?''

"Of course. He bought the property on Hawaii before Mother died. I remember the picnics there and the little house. Does he have the same caretaker? I haven't been over there since long before I went to California.''

''Oh, yes. And he bought next door — that is if twenty-five adjoining acres is next door. The Howard place. The Howards retired there, remember? Then she became ill and he wanted to sell in a hurry. They've gone to a retirement home in Oahu — ''

''But so much land and another house?''

''Yes, and it's bigger and modern. The view is superb — looking toward the distant sea from the front door and the mountain from the back — through a mist of jacaranda.''

''What does Denis think of it?''

''What does an assistant manager think of anything the manager chooses to do? He thinks Greg's out of his head to even consider retiring.''

''But he'll be manager unless something untoward happens.''

''Natch,'' said Lani carelessly and Maggie laughed.

''You treat him wretchedly,'' she said. ''You don't deserve him. But you've had him for years. Old dog Tray.''

"That's right," said Lani cheerfully. "I'm merciless. Please don't tell me that you're sorry for him."

"Of course I'm sorry for him."

"That," said Lani, watching the candles flicker, "is your curse. You're always sorry for everyone. That's what happened to you before you went away — a bad attack of pity."

"Shut up," said Maggie crossly.

"That's all it was, little earth mother who mends broken hearts. You've been in that business since we were kids. But that last time was a glaring mistake."

Maggie said, "Please don't, Lani, I know. . . . You've told me; Greg's told me."

"I'm beginning to learn you can't tell anyone anything. But let me fill you in on our mutual friend Tim. He's made a career of it, Maggie; you've really done him a favor."

"What in the world do you mean?"

"For a week after you left he was heartbroken again. He'd recovered from whatever her name was — but then he had to get over you. So after you — well,

231

there've been a few local idiots and tourist types. Maybe the current one will wind up being Mrs. Heartbroken. She has money.''

Maggie laughed without much conviction. She rose and carried the plates into the kitchen. ''I have ice cream,'' she said, ''also fruit.''

''Just coffee. I ate too much at the wedding festivities. How will I look surfing, when I get back?''

''Gorgeous, as usual. Let's take our coffee to the living room. I'll put things in the dishwasher and bring the coffeepot for seconds.''

Rinsing the bowls, plates, glasses and silver, she thought about Tim Hamilton and shivered. It hadn't been the first time she'd been an idiot, but it was the worst, the most consequential and regrettable, and it was one reason why she wished never to return to the Islands, except perhaps for an occasional visit. Being sorry for Tim had cost her a good deal — her pride, her home, and much of her self-respect. How many times had Lani said, ''But you're not in love with Tim, Maggie; you're just sorry for him.''

"How do you know?" Maggie had once retorted. "I'm sorry for Denis, the way you treat him, but I'm certainly not in love with him."

"Denis," Lani had said, "wouldn't give you the time of day if he had two watches and both running — even if you were in love with him. Tim, of course, is enchanted. When Sybil tossed him, his ego was shattered. So, you've built it up, but he isn't in love with you, honey, whatever he says."

He wasn't. Maggie had found that out. . . .

She heard the car stop, the knock at the door and Lani calling, "Come in unless you mean us harm. Door's open."

She heard someone laugh, went out with a towel in her hands, and said, "Hi, Alan."

"Passing by, as usual; saw the lights; figured you girls were in. Thought you had a dishwasher, Maggie."

"I do. But I don't put my hands in it to dry. Sit down. What may I bring you?"

Lani said gravely, "Maggie's so maternal. Also, she'd make some male chauvinist a marvelous wife. She waits on men, from eight to eighty.''

''And you don't? . . . Thanks, Maggie. I've just had dinner.''

''Certainly not,'' Lani answered with indignation. ''What are men for except to wait on us?''

''Then, may I bring you something?'' Alan asked soberly.

Lani smiled and shook her head. Her heavy lustrous hair swung like a dark bell and he said, ''Please don't think me rude, but your coloring is so unusual.''

''Thus spake the dermatologist,'' Maggie commented.

''Maggie must have told you, I have Hawaiian blood,'' Lani said, ''and a dash of Irish and German. Also there's the Scot who married an ancestress. On my father's side, it's all New England, although he was born in the Islands; his father, a doctor, was also — but the blood is granite, that is to say, New Hampshire; his grandfather came out as a missionary. Actually, I'm more mongrel that I look.''

''I'd hardly call it mongrel,'' Alan objected. ''But I must get on home and report. Lily asked me to stop by and tell you to be sure not to forget Saturday."

"Alan, are you certain we're not imposing on her?" Maggie asked.

"Of course not. She's seeing people again and has been for some time — mostly in connection with the Foundation, and hospital and her other interests."

When he'd gone, Lani said reflectively, "I'm sorry I said that about men from eight to eighty. I imagine he thought of the little boy."

"Oh, I'm certain he didn't. Though Lily might have."

"He's just as shaken as she is, Maggie."

"Yes, I know, but differently, I suppose."

"He's a strange man," Lani commented. "I have an impression he's not at all like his appearance."

"Meaning?"

"I'm not sure. If he looked — well — ordinary or, let's say, average, it would suit him better."

"You make even less sense than usual."

"Not at all. You're dazzled by the appearance. Ninety percent of the time, very unattractive people are utterly unlike what they look like; same goes for beauty. Me, for instance," Lani said, unabashed. "I look like a dream. I ain't."

Maggie laughed. "You're so modest, darling. . . . Come to think of it you really are," she added.

On the next evening they dined with Andrew, Matt, Katie and Jeremy Palmer and, to Maggie's delight, Vanessa.

She said, looking Lani over carefully, "You were born to trouble, of course, but you'll stay out of it."

And Lani said serenely, "I intend to."

Matt was talking to Maggie. "Pop asked Vanessa. He said we should have an extra man, and as he didn't know any unattached males, he with some trepidation, asked Vanessa. He says she's man enough for anyone."

Maggie looked over at Vanessa, smoking one of her thin cigars and regarding Moxie tolerantly. He was lying beside her chair, and Lani remarked, "That's a very handsome dog."

Vanessa frowned. She ruffled her white hair and addressed Maggie in her unique baritone. "There's a flaw in your visitor. She doesn't understand people. Moxie," she informed Lani, "is people, he's not dog, any more than Shadow is cat — that is, except in the ordinary sense. Moxie believes he's people, so does Shadow. I am not very fond of dog-persons generally speaking, but Moxie is a gentleman."

"May I come see your cat-person?" Lani asked politely.

"Certainly. I think you have something in common."

"Cattiness?"

"Of course not. Shadow is not catty; he rarely criticizes, never gossips. He's simply feline by nature. You too."

"She *is* a witch," said Lani to the company at large and Jeremy Palmer, unfolding himself from his chair to accept a second libation, said, "I for one have never doubted it."

Later, at home, Lani told her sister, "I like the Palmers. Katie's a delightful go-getter; Jeremy's a doll. . . . So many attractive men in this hamlet, and all married. Except Matt and I think either he'll marry early — "

"He's not all that young!"

" — and often," Lani continued, "or never. Shall I have time to visit your extraordinary friend Vanessa and her — you'll excuse the expression — cat?"

"Next week. You're not leaving till Thursday. And I wish you'd never go."

"And desert my own, my native land?" asked Lani in horror. "Are you nuts?"

"I don't suppose," Maggie said mournfully, "you'd ever want to live here, but you can visit."

"I promise. In due time I'll bring my husband, and at decent intervals my descendants, who should of course see something of their grandfather's background as well as their father's."

Maggie said, "I think my hair is uncurling — who's the fortunate *kanaka?*"

"Denis, of course."

"Of course! Have you informed him of your game plan?"

"Not as yet." Lani had been sitting on her sister's bed. Now she lay down and flung her arms behind her head. "I think I decided when I was six and he was twelve and told him so. He rejected the idea with violence. In fact, before your mother separated us, he'd slapped my face and pulled my hair. Ever since I was, well, sixteen or fourteen — your guess is as good as mine — I've made him pay for it. But I've always loved him, Maggie."

"Weren't you ever afraid of losing him?" Maggie inquired. "A guy can take just so much."

"Oh, he strayed now and then," Lani admitted, "but not for long."

"I'm amazed, but happy for you," Maggie said. "I love Denis too."

"That's what I was afraid of because I knew you were sorry for him. Thank heaven you're not his type," said Lani. "Anyway, maybe when I get home, I'll tell him I'd like to go to another wedding — ours — around, I think, Christmas. You'd better be there!"

"What a life you'll lead him," Maggie said, "but what a manager's wife you'll make — after assistant manager's!"

"I've been in training all these years," Lani said.

"Does Greg know?"

"Certainly. I told him several years ago and pledged him to secrecy. I said, 'Don't tell Maggie. She'd look from Denis to me, starry-eyed.' Also I said, 'For God's sake, don't tell Denis. He wouldn't believe it — not from you. He'd think it wishful thinking on your part so you'd be sure of appropriate succession!'"

15

Luncheon at the Carstairs' in the elegant, restored house was informal and pleasant. Maggie and Lani were the only guests, and Alan came in very briefly to say hello. He had appointments, and when he was through in the office, he had to go to the city in a consultant capacity.

"He rarely gets home for lunch nowadays," said Lily, "but then, I'm out quite often." She smiled at Lani. "It's a little disturbing," she added, "that so many meetings for charitable purposes are luncheons, even dinners."

This was a house, Lani thought — as they moved from the dining room to the living room — replete with charm, excellent taste and the money to indulge it. Nothing was elaborate or ostentatious, everything — old or new — was good. The colors were right — Lani was very knowledgeable about color — the paintings, originals; the housekeeping meticulous. Lily spoke of the Islands, remembering some of the places, also flowers and trees, by their original names.

Lani was astonished. She looked at her sister and said, *"Mahalo!"*

Lily, smiling, asked, "Doesn't that mean thank you?"

"Oh yes, but it's also an exclamation of amazement."

"It's not remarkable," Lily told her. "I brought home from our first trip a small dictionary and I looked at it just this morning. So I cheated. But I've always been fascinated by languages. I speak three beside our own — Spanish, French and German — not well, but I can get along; and I've a smattering of Italian. . . . I know I haven't a natural ear, but that was the way I was brought up. . . ."

When they were ready to leave, Lily said, "Maggie, I've missed you. Do come see me again soon. Alan has told me how kind you've been every time he stopped to see you."

The warmth was there, Maggie thought, but it was turned on, like a sun lamp, a radiator, an oven.

When she and Lani were back home, Maggie said, "I'm glad Lily's going out and seeing people, but I wish you'd known her before Kim was killed, Lani. She was so — well, spontaneously outgoing. She was beautiful when she smiled. Now, it seems so empty."

"She goes through the motions," Lani agreed. "The doctor must make a vault full of dough to maintain the house, and such food bills — I certainly didn't expect fresh caviar with that gorgeous sherry — to say nothing of the servants and his wife's clothes."

Maggie said reluctantly, "Lily inherited a great deal of money, Lani. I'm sure Alan earns a lot now, but it takes time. They married before he was in practice."

"That's obvious," Lani said. "He's at least ten years younger than she is. No wonder she's so stricken by the loss of the boy; she probably won't have another child."

"No," said Maggie. "She can't. She told

243

me so." She looked at Lani, stretched in one of Aunt Hattie's lawn chairs under a big maple, and added, "Actually she has one."

"Alan?"

"Alan?"

"He's lost without her," Maggie said. "So dependent — I don't mean money."

"What did she mean he came to see you? . . . Oh, he has since I arrived — with the flowers — but otherwise?"

"He had to talk to someone," Maggie said.

"Redheads have such sensitive skins," Lani remarked, "to their sorrow. I don't, thank heaven. There you go again being sorry for someone. The odd thing is it's rarely a female."

Maggie flung her hands apart in exasperation. "Everyone fell in love with him, Lani — including me, a little. I saw quite a lot of him and Lily — of Kim too. We went skiing. Matt took me first. The Carstairs were at the Lodge. Later I went with them. I wrote you all about it."

"Some of it certainly, but skiing isn't exactly your bag," said Lani. "I was mildly astonished. However, I thought it was your New England blood egging you on to broken bones. . . . So having been, as you say, slightly in love, you progressed to the more deadly emotion — pity."

"I'm over that," said Maggie. "I mean, as a threat to my security — like Tim," she added painfully. "I've been told several times that Alan's crazy about his wife and believed it, but I didn't realize until recently that he's actually more dependent than Kim ever was. That boy was a rugged individual. I used to watch him — and marvel. He loved his parents, but his personality was his own. There were physical resemblances, of course, but that's all. He wasn't a child, at ten; he was a man in miniature — except in the obvious ways — at his age very self-reliant. Alan, I've discovered, isn't."

"Lily doesn't appear to know it," said Lani, tiring a little of other people's problems, even Maggie's. "Someone ought to tell her so. . . . Let's talk about me. Isn't it marvelous to live in a place where you can count on the weather? We'll be married on the *lanai*. If you don't fly over for it, Maggie, I'll kill myself and haunt you forever.''

"I'm boring you?'' Maggie asked.

"Well, yes. I do wish you wouldn't go around like the late lamented Sherlock with a magnifying glass, examining your friends and enemies for treasure, flaws or whatever. I expected you to be more enthralled than you are by the prospect of me marrying Denis.''

"I'm enthralled,'' siad Maggie. "Believe it. I'm also scared — that you'll change your mind.''

"Never.''

"You have before.''

"Oh come, Maggie. I was never serious. It was fun and games while it lasted and I couldn't be hurt. You know that. But I've been serious about Denis since childhood. I simply wasn't willing to settle down. You, on the contrary, have been ready for some time, but you always look in the wrong direction.''

"What's that supposed to mean?''

"Look up the hill. Matt.''

"Good grief,'' said Maggie, stunned. "Matt?''

"What's wrong with him?"

"Nothing. He's a field player, he's as little anxious to — as you call it — settle down as you used to be. He likes me fine and isn't interested in me at all, nor I in him. I've told you so."

"Certainly. And you haven't made any effort to get his attention. All he knows is you like him fine too — and his dog, better. I give up."

"You'd better," Maggie said.

Dinner that night with Matt was in a costly place in Saltmarsh — very French, very good. Lani exclaimed over it. "In New England?" she marveled.

"We have everything," Matt said. "How about the Islands?"

"Oh everything's there too — if you look for it. But this is quite fantastic. Sure you can afford it?" Lani inquired.

"No. But I've already collected some campaign funds for printing, advertising, posters, radio and the like and to what better use can I put it?"

"Spoken like a man and politician. I note Maggie seems unimpressed, even blasé!"

"I've been here before," Maggie said, "with the Palmers and their friends, Ross Cameron and his wife."

"Always wives! Who are they?"

"Comparative newcomers," Matt explained.

"Everyone's a newcomer," Maggie commented, "any time after, say, seventeen hundred."

"Beth Cameron is beautiful," Matt went on serenely. "He's rich, also very likable; he's an old friend of Jeremy Palmer. He bought a house in Little Oxford through Katie — one with a history and a swimming pool. Sorry they're not here now, but they travel a lot. You'd like them, Lani. You could hold your own with Beth — who once worked for Jeremy in the bookshop — and I believe the urge to pursue has left Cam, since his marriage."

"I didn't know it left any man," Maggie remarked.

"It's gone out of me," Matt said gloomily. "Too expensive, too time-consuming, too tiring. From now on in, I'll sit with my law books, drinking and brooding, companioned by Moxie.''

On the following Tuesday, Maggie took Lanie to Vanessa's for supper. She said, "She's a gourmet cook, better than the *Chez Nous* at Saltmarsh. She doesn't often do this for anyone. Her great friends here are Lee and Stacy Osborne — you've met them. Stacy took me to see her originally. Vanessa's been to the Islands, Lani, so don't be startled if she implies some great romance took place there. One has, I think, in every place she's ever been except here.''

Lani was fascinated by Vanessa's cluttered living room. "It's a parlor really," Vanessa told her, "and I still keep my odds and ends as you see. Dust catchers. When my grandson has to sort my memories, he'll have a rough time; they'll all belong to him, with the exception of a few things which Ben and Bing and others might like — "

"Please don't talk like that," Maggie begged her. "Look at Shadow; he's just sitting, staring at Lani.''

So he was — erect, his tail curled about

his paws, his great emerald eyes fixed upon the stranger. Maggie, he accepted. He had shrugged slightly when she entered, a friendly gesture of hospitality.

"He's admiring you," Vanessa explained. "He's also recognizing your quality. Does he make you nervous, Lani?"

"No," said Lani, and smiled at Shadow who smiled back and then went to lie beside Vanessa. "He's waiting for his aperitif," Vanessa explained. "Maggie will help me, you look around. There's a feather lei over there somewhere, in one of the whatnots."

It was a beautiful one, and Lani looked at it with envy. She had a couple herself, which she used on her big straw hats, but none as fine as this. Maggie and Vanessa came in with trays — sherry and biscuits — and Lani said, "You bought this in the Islands, of course?"

"It was given to me there," said Vanessa. "I wore it for some time on a hat."

"It's a very special lei," Lani told her.

"Of course," said Vanessa carelessly.

They dined on chicken, mushrooms and rice in a casserole, white wine, fresh asparagus and for a sweet, fruit. Then coffee and cordials and Vanessa said suddenly, "You were distressed, Maggie, because I spoke of death?"

"I suppose so. I didn't mean to interrupt you, Mrs. Steele, I'm sorry."

"My friends call me Van. Somehow, since Stacy and I became friends, I've enjoyed young people more than I ever have since I was young. Before I knew Stacy my interest in this generation was mainly in my grandson Adam. If he ever saw you, Lani, he'd — I believe it's called flip."

"Alas," said Lani, "he must be much too young for me."

"I don't know," Vanessa said. "He's out of college, away in Europe. When he comes back, I suppose he'll go into banking. Maggie, the reason I spoke as I did is that at my age you think a great deal about dying. You know, of course, that you will experience it — that's what it is — an experience, like birth or love. You know it, so you think about it and you arrange things in a law office, at a bank or in your mind. But actually, you don't believe it will ever be *your* experience. You know it, you don't believe it. It will happen to everyone on this planet but yourself. When you reach my age — or even before — you'll realize this; maybe you'll remember. . . . Now, in twenty minutes Shadow will escort you to the door. I tire easily."

Maggie said, "But you haven't let us wash up, Van."

"I've a pleasant enough girl coming in the morning," Vanessa said. "Everything's ready for her. I'm thinking of asking her to stay with me. I'm sick of fighting doctors and relatives. It will mean an adjustment for me and Shadow — he likes her, thank God — but also for her. We'll see. . . . Lani, I'm giving you the feather lei."

"You mustn't," Lani exclaimed, horrified, but touched. "You don't even know me!"

"My dear child," Vanessa said sharply, "what difference does that make? Most of the people I know I wouldn't give a tinker's damn to — or for — and it's appropriate for you. You're getting married soon — "

"How did you know that?" Lani demanded.

"Oh, so you are? . . . Well, it isn't hard to predict. Any young woman who looks like you could never escape past, say the age of twenty-three or four unless she selected more unconventional alliances. In any case, he's probably an Islander."

"Repeating my question — " Lani began.

"Not necessary. I doubt you'd want to live elsewhere. Go fetch the lei. After you're married, give it to your husband to wear around his hat."

Lani held it with reverence. Leis, mostly pheasant feathers like this, had cost in the hundreds thirty-five years ago and were very difficult to come by now.

Shadow took them to the door, and Vanessa spoke from her straight-backed chair, "Come as often as you please, Maggie," she said. "You can call me — I have a telephone now." She explained to Lani, "I didn't until rather recently, when I was forced to install the instrument of torture — one upstairs, one down." She added balefully, "For a while I wouldn't answer it. I thought I need use it only to scream for help but I found if I didn't answer, people came rushing over fearing — maybe even hoping — to find me with a broken hip or shattered skull — "

"Van," Maggie said gently, "stop that kind of talk or I'll break your arm!"

"All right. Affectionate regards to Andrew and Matt," Vanessa said. "Shadow greets the courteous canine."

"That," said Lani, as they got into the car, "is one of the most fascinating females I ever met. Is she really as much of a recluse as she implies?"

"No. She's very close to Stacy and Lee Osborne. Turns up now and then at the Palmers', and was, if you'll remember, at Matt's — she's a client of his father's. She's quite a pal of the farmers up the road from her; she sees Rosie Niles now and then — you don't know her, I'm sorry to say — and of course the Irvingtons. When Van came back here to live, years ago, and bought the house, no one really knew her. Now, of course, even if you don't know her, you know of her, and Shadow."

"That cat scares me."

"But we've always had cats, Lani."

"Not like this one. Ours are purry, tabby types. We still have a couple. My respected parent calls them 'Come' and 'Go' and that's all they do."

"But he named the goldfish that!"

"Now they're the cats' names, by osmosis and I really mean it. Dad said after they'd eaten the last of the clan, he'd rather have cats; they are somewhat more lovable even if destructive."

Lani left Wednesday. She had a stopover with friends in San Francisco.

"If I could bear to live off the Islands, it would be there," she explained to Matt.

She was taking a late-afternoon flight and he was driving her and Maggie to the airport.

"Promise me," he had said, "swear to me, Magpie, you won't cry. If you do, I'll leave you at home, and maybe Lani and I will elope."

"You deserve each other," Maggie had told him.

"Actually," he said after he'd loaded them and the luggage into the car, "this is no hardship. Dad's taking my appointments. I have two, both with fairly attractive, very well-heeled women who want out of their respective marriages. He loathes divorce cases; what he despises most is listening to the various high-pitched, mercenary complaints. I know. I've had both couples in my office at various time for the well-known stab at reconciliation. It's part of our friendly service," he explained graciously, "and stab is really the word. One couple bickered over custody of the poodle; the other, if faltering memory serves me, over a water bed. Scotch and water, I think, actually. No one fought over the children. Fifty-fifty . . . take your turn, bribe the unfortunate offspring then send them back to Mom or Poppa as the vacation ends. One reason I refuse to marry is I couldn't mount a quarrel which could lead to divorce; I'd fight to the teeth for Moxie, and I don't want kids."

"I hope I live to see you eat those words, plain or with Hollandaise," Lani said.

"Plain, please. I have to watch my figure and my cholesterol."

"In the meantime," Maggie suggested, "watch your driving."

"You see! I appeal to you, Lani. . . . If I had a wife, that would be one of her battle cries."

"And the others?" Maggie asked.

"Watch your weight. Don't watch other women. Watch your spending. Don't watch mine. Watch your drinking. Watch my hairdo and lipstick. Watch out for my new unruffled dress."

"Who'd marry him?" Maggie asked Lani.

"Dozens," Lani responded promptly. "You know we're in the minority."

Nearing the airport, Maggie said, "I don't think I can stand watching you go, Lani."

"You won't watch her," said Matt. "I won't. We'll drop her off; a porter will oblige and we won't have to see her — straight-backed, head high and courageous — walk through the doors without looking back. Just remember her as she is now. Or else go with her, stowing away if necessary. Emotional women make me nervous."

The car slid to a miraculous halt in front of the particular airline. "Stay there," Lani commanded. She kissed each briskly, imperiously beckoned a porter, who, also miraculously, arrived on the run — and she was gone.

"Now cry," Matt told her resignedly, as he prepared to fight his way back into the traffic. "I suggest we eat on the road, near home. I know a singles' bar. I'm sure you've never been to one. Actually it isn't entirely singles, just the cocktail lounge, which is haunted by hopefuls. There are ordinary tables and comfortable chairs and excellent food. . . . You aren't crying. How come?"

"I was thinking, it's a good thing I don't have more guests from exotic lands. The hospital will never be the same. I dragged Lani up there one morning — she went back home by taxi — and this is the second time they let me off early. But now she's gone, I don't know what to do."

"See your friends, do your job, entertain, have an affair."

"With whom?"

"Well, not with me. I can't afford it. I could however, if you insist, marry you, Magpie."

"Are you off your rocker?"

"I must be even to consider it. But I'm sorry for you" — he favored her with a sidelong glance — "and you know how it is when you're sorry for people."

"You," said Maggie, "are impossible!"

"Good. I take it you refuse me."

"In spades."

"Then I'll buy you two drinks, although actually I figure marriage, costly as it is, is less expensive than the occasional girl or girls. Beats me why they want to be liberated. The liberties they take with the poor idiots who buy flowers, wine, meals and weekends are appalling."

"We'll go Dutch tonight," said Maggie with dignity.

"No. I would find it embarrassing. Male chauvinistic pride, of course. I'll keep an expense account, however, or take it out in time."

"What kind of time?"

"Campaign time; you can make phone

calls, type letters — be, in fact, my left hand. I have to save my right for the handshaking."

"Thanks a heap," said Maggie. "Do you really think you have the personality to win your little election?"

"Disdain it not. Certainly. I am rugged, forthright, masculine, agreeable. I love animals. I tolerate other people's children. I can answer questions. I have Moxie, man's best friend, to protect me. I'm going to teach him how to manipulate a voting machine. I am a lawyer, which does not, of course, make me Caesar's wife. On the other hand my father, also a lawyer, has a very high reputation. Andrew Comstock's son has to be honest; also he'll have no temptation to tiptoe through the till. I don't tell my girls that usually. I do very well by them but sigh when I look at dinner checks. . . . It wouldn't do to supply them with credit ratings, but seeing that you are not my girl, I'll confide in you. You'll be lonely evenings and weekends without our gorgeous guest — what's the Hawaiian generic appellation?"

"*Wahini.*"

"Sounds better than 'woman,' which can be spoken in a variety of ways. Of course, for those who prefer no spoken distinction between the sexes, 'person' is popular. . . . Who's Denis?"

"The man Lani's planning to marry. Why?"

"You sent him your best love — and to Greg. But I know who Greg is. I simply wondered if you had someone languishing on the beach. When's Lani getting married?"

"She thinks around Christmas." Maggie laughed. "But Denis doesn't know about it yet. You see, he's been trailing her since they were kids. She always knew he'd catch up one day, but until now she has preferred her freedom. I'll never get off for Christmas, Matt," she added sorrowfully.

"Maybe, for a week. You'll have been at the hospital a little more than a year by the time wedding bells and carols ring out. Dad's on the Board. Lots of Boards. So if you lose your job, he'll get you another. I might consider a short holiday myself and fly out with you to make sure you return. On the other hand, I cannot desert my parent and Moxie at Yuletide. Did you ever look up your father's people in Deeport, Maggie?"

"Your father did. There's a distant cousin, of this generation. He's a banker, and his wife's an old friend of Katie Palmer's. She's promised to take me to call. Aunt Hattie, your father thinks, knew Tom Davis's parents and probably him."

"So small the world," said Matt. "Now put on your lipstick. I'll slow to a walk; blot away what's left of the tears as, in a few minutes, I'll usher you into the appropriately singles' bar. After which we'll go home. Moxie's mad at me. I haven't taken him with me lately. Either my destination was tabu for dog people or too dull or inhabited by other household pets, all unfriendly. I've told him next time he finds himself alone to go and spend the evening with you."

"But he generally does," said Maggie.

Matt shook his head. "He never breathed a word of this to me," he said. "When I reach home, he's always there, smugly sleeping with one ear cocked, just waiting patiently for me . . . I thought."

16

July was hot and there were a good many accidents on back roads and highways. The emergency room and the medical and nursing staff were busy and beds were hard to find.

People not only had accidents but illnesses, and there were to be numerous additions to the population. Maggie was busy too. Mrs. Cromwell lent her to various departments to help out when people had vacations.

"Is it always like that?" Maggie asked Amy. They were not at Amy's but at Rosie Niles's. Mrs. Niles wasn't home, but her pool was kept fresh and clean for those of her friends who cared to use it. On this afternoon, Katie was there also. Jeremy was working. Ben was working. Katie wasn't. She had given Nanny the day off to visit an air-conditioned relative and she and Amy had their small fry with them, closely guarded.

"Well," Amy answered, "Little Oxford's not a resort, of course, but we are not far from public and private beaches. People do drown or step on rusty nails or get sunburned, and those who romp carelessly through the fields have poison ivy. There's also that summer flu bug in addition to other common ailments. Ben's up to his ears and Bing's so tired Letty's threatened to leave him if he doesn't take a vacation. However, it will simmer down. There are lots of summer residents here. You know, people go away and rent their houses at astronomical prices for a month, two, even three months. And then we have residents who are here from April or May only to October or November. Well, not actually here — often at the ocean or in the mountains. They winter like the birds in far-flung islands or the South, but their houses are kept habitable in case there's an emergency or they decide to rough it at home. . . . By the way, didn't you two go to Deeport this morning?"

"Oh yes, Linda was so glad to see me

and Benjy — and to meet Maggie and introduce her to the baby,'' Katie answered.

"Girl or boy?"

"Girl. At the moment I prefer boys but, second time around, perhaps I won't. Anyway, Tom came home for lunch; we had what's known as a repast. Linda has someone now who comes in and helps when needed. I haven't seen her since young Julia arrived three months ago. . . . Jeremy and I saw her, then, at the hospital.''

"Weren't you looking for relatives, Maggie?'' Amy asked.

"Found them. Seems Tom's father really was related to mine — it's not a close connection but it was fun to talk about it . . . and he did know Aunt Hattie, though he hadn't seen her in years.''

"You must miss Lani,'' Katie said.

"I do. But frankly,'' Maggie said, in some astonishment, "not as much as I thought I would. I suppose I've put down roots here.'' She smiled at her friends and young Benjy waddled up and clutched her firmly by the legs. "You're starting young," she told him, then continued, "Actually I hadn't seen much of Lani in recent years. She was away at college, of course, home for summers and holidays; then I went to California and flew home only on short vacations. I love her dearly," she added, "but apparently I can function without her — even without Greg, though when I first came here I didn't think it possible."

When Katie dropped Maggie off at the house, Moxie was waiting, lying down sedately, his paws crossed and Katie said, "I see you have a follower."

"Matt must be off for the weekend. Moxie gets lonely. Probably Mr. Comstock's playing golf and Mrs. Hunt's out shopping. . . . Thanks, Katie. I had a lovely day."

"Not planning to go out again?"

"No, this is a wash the hair, manicure the nails, read a good book night, I think. Also, feed and comfort Moxie."

She stood there, the slanting sun on her red hair and her freckles marching across her nose and high cheekbones. She was brown again now after the winter during which her tan had faded. And Katie drove off thinking how pretty she looked and how annoyed Mrs. Warner was because she, Katie, had taken two days off, but she'd be all right on Monday. "Besides," Katie told herself, "the hot weather slump's on. Things will pick up in the autumn and in the meantime I'll have a little time to spend with the Jeremy's."

Shortly after eight that evening, Maggie emerged from under the hair drier which she had given herself at Easter. She was wearing a cotton slip, a cotton kimono and mules. There wasn't, she reflected, much percentage in an electric drier at this point, as it made her hotter. She took her manicuring tools and went downstairs; the kitchen was cooler tonight than any room except Aunt Hattie's, and, except for coffee, her supper had not required the stove.

Sitting at the table with a towel under her hands and a small bowl of soapy hot water nearby, she reflected upon a number of matters, none important. Moxie might have stayed with her she thought, but no, he must have had psychic knowledge that Matt would be home soon since, directly after his supper, he'd indicated, smiling, that he'd had a pleasant evening and then pointed himself toward the door.

When the knock came, she thought: That's Matt and was astonished to realize she'd missed him. Then, remembering what Lani had said, was suddenly enraged. She had a telephone. He could make use of it. She also had a rather soothing chiming bell. Why therefore knock the door down? When the summons was repeated, she went to the door, muttering crossly to herself.

"It was open," she began . . . but it wasn't Matt; it was Alan Carstairs.

"You shouldn't leave it unlocked," he reproached her. "May I come in?"

"Yes . . . but I'm not really in the mood for gentlemen callers. This is my hair and hands night."

"I'm just here with a message. Lily asked me to stop by and see if you'd come for tea and a swim tomorrow, about four? We haven't been using the pool much," he added.

They'd built it, Maggie knew, for Kim.

"I'd like to, Alan," she said. "I've a brunch date so I'll be home by two."

"Well, thanks," he said. "I'll tell her," and went on, walking in the abstracted manner she'd noticed these past months, his normally straight shoulders sagging.

Why did she send him here? She could have called me herself, Maggie thought.

Sunday brunch was some miles away at an excellent tavern high on a ridge. Mrs. Cromwell had asked Maggie and two executives from the nursing staff. She'd explained to Maggie, "I feel it's time I had a small party. You and Joan and Gwen have bought me innumerable cups of coffee all winter and spring."

Matt turned up with Moxie about eleven on Sunday and inquired, "Like me to take you somewhere, or would you favor fixing a salad and iced coffee here say at noon?"

"I've a date. Thanks just the same."

"How about supper?"

"I'll be at the Carstairs' for a swim about four; home, I'm sure, in a couple of hours, but I have no desire to cater. It's hot and, while I had yesterday and today off, I'm still wrung out."

Matt smote her upon her bottom. He said, "Fragile and complaining girls repel me, and don't look affronted. If you were in Italy, you'd be really insulted if you weren't whacked or pinched."

"I'm not in Italy and you hurt!"

"Nonsense. About this evening" — he looked at Moxie who winked at him — "we'll compromise. Be home by six. Mrs. Hunt will provide nourishment and it will cost us nothing. You save; I save. I've no idea why, when I work so hard for a buck, I become entangled with expensive women. It must be psychological. . . . Heard from Lani?"

"She telephoned from the Coast."

"Now there's an extravagant lass . . . in every way. I trust her Denis is loaded."

"No. He does have some inherited money, but he lives on his salary."

"I'm horrified. How will she cope?"

"Lani always copes, no matter what."

"It isn't possible, looking as she does. . . . See you around six. Think you can drag yourself up the hill or shall I call for you?"

"I'll walk." Suddenly she was sorry for him. "I'm sure the Carstairs would like you to come with me," she said.

"I dislike pools. I'll head for the Turners'. They have the private beach I keep forgetting to take you to. Be seein' you, Magpie."

She thought: Now why was I sorry for *him?* He has dozens of friends, hundreds for all I know, statewide, with beaches and pools, probably a few Olympic ones. But he looked sort of beat, and I think troubled.

Brunch was fun. They ate it on a wide cool veranda. Maggie liked Joan, who was about forty, a lean brown woman, and also Gwen, younger, prettier and just as efficient.

At the table the conversation inevitably centered around the hospital.

"Dr. Carstairs," Gwen sighed. "He doesn't come in much, of course. His wife's a volunteer. I suppose you know that, Maggie."

"Oh, yes. She didn't tell me, but someone did."

"She won't work in the children's ward anymore," Joan said. "She won't even go in it. Personally, I think it's morbid. Helping other children — that would be good therapy. Most of the volunteers love to. They read to them and play with the smaller ones if they're well enough."

Mrs. Cromwell said thoughtfully, "I daresay no one understands another person's grief."

"But it's unhealthy," Joan persisted.

Gwen, a decade her junior, shook her head. "You're a hard gal," she said, "and you don't have children. None of us has. How could we possibly understand Mrs. Carstairs?"

"We're fortunate," Mrs. Cromwell said, "our children are in their late teens. By the time my husband and I retire, we shall, hopefully, have grandchildren."

Maggie arriving at the Carstairs', walking from the car to the house, admired the landscaping — a trifle elegant, far better manicured than her nails and by a professional. She admired the garden, well watered; the summer flowers and the grass under the diffused spray. The patio around the pool had great pots of geraniums at each corner, bright lounge chairs, big cushions and water as blue as the sky. No one was out there under the umbrellas and when she rang and was admitted, Lily came into the square hall to meet her. "I hope you brought your suit," she said.

"I certainly did — cap, robe, towel and swim slippers too. Aren't you going in?"

"I think not. I'll be outside with you though. We'll have tea there, or coffee — iced or hot?" she asked.

"Coffee," decided Maggie, "and cold."

"I expected Alan," Lily said, "but he's off somewhere." For a moment a shadow crossed her face. "He's restless as a bird." She added, "Here's the little dressing room right off the pool. Don't be afraid to drip back. I'll just get my hat."

Lily came out, sat under a green-and-white umbrella, on a matching chaise with a table beside her, and watched Maggie swim. Now and then she made a comment.

"Like a tropical fish," she said once.

"From about four," Maggie said. "I was

three when my mother remarried and went to the Islands."

"I'd forgotten Lani was your stepsister."

"I forgot that from the time we met," said Maggie. She came up the steps, put on her robe and sat on the edge of the pool.

"She's a beautiful girl," Lily said, "and such vitality. I imagine she is more than merely popular."

"Ever since she was six," said Maggie, "her male following filled our house, the beach, the grounds. By the time she was sixteen they would have crowded a small auditorium." She laughed, her eyes as bright as the sky-reflecting pool.

Lily asked, "Were you never envious?"

"Oh, not really," Maggie said cheerfully. "I didn't exactly lack for heartbreaking — it was usually my head," she admitted.

"I grew up envious," Lily said. "A second cousin used to stay with us, and I hated her. I could have killed her. She was very lovely at that time — not now. She's ten years older than I and has had a lot of trouble — husband, children." The shadow was back briefly. "Alan had a beautiful sister. I never knew her. I did know his mother. She aged prematurely. She had worked always, and very hard."

"Alan spoke of her to me," Maggie said.

"You've helped him a great deal."

"I just let him talk," Maggie said.

A maid came with a frosty pitcher, glasses and delectable cookies and Lily asked, "Perhaps you'd rather have a drink? How thoughtless of me . . . but that's usually Alan's job."

"No, thanks," Maggie told her. "I'm going out to dinner and perhaps by then I can face a stimulant."

"You're facing two now; tea for me, coffee for you. Both stimulants, if nonalcoholic. I sound like a stewardess. . . . Now come and have your coffee," Lily said.

Maggie stood, toweling her hair for a moment, then sat down in the lounge chair opposite her hostess. "This," she announced, "is the life."

"Part of it," Lily agreed. She added suddenly, "I can't sleep; not for long, even when I take the capsules Alan prescribes.

He's very careful to see I never have many, but he needn't worry. Even if I took that way out, I wouldn't be with Kim." She looked at Maggie, her eyes empty in the blunt little face. "If what we are taught is true," she said, "it would be a sin . . . and if it isn't true, there's nothing but oblivion."

Maggie said, distressed, "I don't believe in oblivion, Lily. There'd be no point in being born. I think you have to go on — everyone does." She hesistated. "Kim has," she said firmly.

After an interval of silence, Lily said bleakly, "I could live twenty years, twenty-five, even more. I'm a healthy woman, physically. If what you believe — and you're fortunate — is true, we wouldn't know one another."

"I believe we would. Perhaps I've been conditioned by the Islands. It's easy to believe in wonders and spiritual awareness there. Lani and I were once in a burial cave during a storm — we heard the drums."

Lily wasn't listening. She said, "Alan has suggested that we adopt a child. I don't want to — I — I can't."

Maggie put down her glass and pulled her robe about her. She thought: I'm scared, but all right, here goes!

"Lily, you have a child," she said.

Lily stared, her color fading. She seemed to shrink, she was sallow and old. "What are you trying to say?"

"Alan."

"Alan!" Lily's eyes widened. "I . . . don't understand."

"He's talked to me," Maggie said. "He needed to; he's lost without you — lost because you've shut him out."

"He told you that!"

"He's wholly dependent on you, a great deal more than Kim was," Maggie went on steadfastly. "Kim loved you and his father — he would have always. That he does still is my belief. But he would have grown up, followed his own life as anyone must, and become independent. I'm not talking about money," Maggie said, flushing, "but about emotional dependence. Kim was a strong little boy; you're a strong woman. Alan isn't strong. He," said Maggie, greatly daring, "is a leaner and when he looked for

277

you to lean on, you simply weren't there.''

"I suppose you were?" Lily asked acidly.

"No . . . no one could be except you."

"Women have always been in love with him," Lily told her.

"Certainly," Maggie agreed, "all of them in this area have been, or are, a little. I was no exception — briefly. But, you see, I'm not interested in a leaner. One of my worst traits is being sorry for people — usually men — and mistaking it for something else which becomes instant disillusionment. I was sorry for Alan after the accident, but not sorry enough to think I could be of any help, in any way. It's you he needs, Lily — for the rest of your lives together."

Lily said, her voice so low Maggie had to strain to hear her, "All our lives together I've been afraid. Afraid of other women. I never showed it; he never knew. The thought that he'd ever realize I was terrified and possessive frightened me even more. So I walked on eggs. I have never been quite sure if I bought him wholly or partly; nor how much I paid.

Kim — Kim was something else. I didn't buy him."

"I think you did," Maggie said haltingly. "I think, in a sense, we all buy what we love and pay a price. You've been paying yours. Greg — Lani's father — used to tell us that no one owns anyone — ever — and all loving exacts a price. It isn't the same for everyone."

She rose. She said, "If I've hurt you, Lily, I'm sorry. You and Alan have been kind to me. Kim and I were friends too, and I'm sorry that I couldn't help Alan but there was no possible way. You're the only one who can. If you don't, I suppose he will destroy himself, one way or another. I think you have provided the only security he has ever known. His profession, his success, or money haven't brought him that. Only you have, in yourself."

She went back to the little dressing room, and packed her small carryall with the two bright pieces of swim gear, towel, robe and slippers, then dressed and went out to her car. She did not see Lily anywhere.

Well, that's that, she thought. Greg

always remarked that my efforts — especially when I was sure I could solve other people's problems — were well intentioned; and, then, reminded me of what road was paved with what. I couldn't help being sorry for Alan and Lily, but I've had a tough course in learning to recognize weakness in myself and others, and I guess only recently could I be given a passing mark.

Driving home, she thought: Well, I'll forget it, dress, walk up the hill to the Comstocks'. Good and uncomplicating friends — Andrew, Matt, Mrs. Hunt and, of course, Moxie.

17

July dutifully became August, the nights were cooler and there was rain, washing the dusty drooping leaves. And Alan Carstairs turned his practice over to his two confreres and he and Lily went away — a cruise, a stay in Copenhagen and another ship home again.

Maggie went horseback riding. Matt had said, "I assume that you ride?" and when she'd answered, "Of course," he had announced that he had a friend who owned horses, and kept them at a local Hunt Club — "not that anyone hunts," — and that he was welcome to use them whenever he wished. So perhaps on a Saturday or Sunday she'd care to go along, "... always provided you don't fall off. I faint at the sight of blood," he warned.

"I'll try to spare your delicate feelings. Somehow you don't look like a horseman, Matt.''

"I'm not bowlegged, if that's what you mean, but I've ridden since I was a kid. My mother had farm relatives upstate. I've never made it to Madison Square, however, or to the local horse shows. . . . And I haven't had much time in recent years. Also my usual female companions prefer cars to equines . . . I've never been fortunate enough to date one of those televised cover gals who gallop up and down the Caribbean beaches,'' he said sadly.

So they rode together companionably on a couple of agreeable steeds, Matt in slacks and Maggie in jeans and both in brilliant shirts.

Moxie stayed docilely in the car, with plenty of air and water and Matt explained, "I'd let him run with us, but maybe the horses are nervous.''

"There's always a dog in a racehorse's stall, isn't there, for company?''

"So I've heard. However I'm taking no chances with someone else's animals. Ben Foley has half a dozen places scattered around and six horses here. . . . We draw the sedate ones, of course, not the show horses."

"You know the darnedest people."

"From rags to riches, and back again. It's probably my profession. Everyone requires a lawyer at one or another time for something. Also, although it may not show, I did attend an elementary school, a boarding school and a university. So I got to meet people. Ben's not from this area, he just has a place beyond the club. He isn't there now, which suits me."

"You don't like him?"

"I like him fine, but he's a lecherous old man."

"Old?"

"At least ten years my senior. Been married three, four times." They were walking their horses and he looked sidewise at her. "Don't you dare feel sorry for him, Magpie."

"Why should I?"

"Oh, 'He's a poor, disillusioned, unlucky-in-love, misunderstood guy' is written all over your face — "

"You're being absurd — no, not entirely. I do feel a kind of compassion for the losers and a lot for any kids involved."

"Ben has several," he told her. "A couple of his ex-wives have not remarried — so there's alimony; one, however, has latched on to a man who can afford her. . . . Why are you scowling?"

"I hate cynicism."

"Realistic, is all. Someday I'll be glad to give you a private seminar on alimony, when it's justified and when it isn't. Child support, of course, is necessary."

"Spare me."

"Okay, but you never know and I do want you to be prepared."

They rode several times thereafter. Maggie enjoyed it.

"It's different," she told Matt, "from the Islands, and the beaches, the mountain trails are different from the few times I rode in California, but great fun. The ridges are beautiful," she added, as they halted their horses at an empty, railed lookout, early one Sunday morning. "I can't wait for the leaves to turn. I was too late for that last year."

By September, Matt was very occupied — in and out of court, in and out of the office. A shop had moved from a second-story office on Chestnut, and Matt moved in temporarily. "Headquarters," he announced, "for a handful of us."

"What happens after Election?" Maggie asked at dinner one night at the Comstocks'.

"Another small business moves in."

"I mean to you."

"I'll lose," Matt told her cheerfully.

Mrs. Hunt, passing by with gravy, said, "You won't do any such thing!"

"I'll vote for you," Maggie assured him.

"Votes count up," he said gravely.

"Then why your negative thinking?" Maggie asked.

"I'll tell you why," his father answered. "He's a trifle too liberal for Little Oxford."

"I can't decide," Matt said, "if I'm a liberal conservative or a conservative liberal. But I'm not discouraged. As the years advance, so will my home town, even if at a snail's pace. Even Little Oxford must change, if not entirely."

"It will," his father assured him. "Perhaps when my generation departs."

Maggie shivered, "I wish people wouldn't talk like that," she said.

"Like what? And who?"

"You for one. Vanessa for another."

"Death is a fact of life, Maggie. However, Van's older than I, but she will probably outlive anyone now turning fifty. She's an incredibly hardy soul. The only setback I can recall her suffering since she came here was a broken arm. Do you see her often, Maggie?"

"Only now and then. I wish I did a lot more. I'm crazy about her and, to my astonishment, about her cat. Last time I was there, Shadow was annoyed with her and was asleep in the linen closet with, of course, the door ajar. I went to call, he opened one green eye, emitted a reluctant purr and went back to sleep."

"Moxie brooks no rivals, you know," Matt said.

"He has none," Maggie answered, smiling.

They returned to the living room where Andrew put a log on the fire and they sat near it with their coffee. Mrs. Hunt came in too. It was "just family" to her way of thinking. She had tea and knitted and Matt said, "It's only mid-October and it can turn very warm again, Maggie. Fall, I think, is my favorite season. Come deep winter we'll all look back and marvel how short the summer and autumn were."

"It's incredible," Maggie said, "that I will have been here a year in November. Lani keeps writing that I've lost whatever mind I ever had. Not that she didn't like Little Oxford and the people she met, especially all present, and she keeps implying that I should pursue and cultivate my opportunities."

"What opportunities?" Matt demanded.

"You."

"Merciful God!"

"That shook him," said his father.

"I daresay Lani's right," Maggie said, raking back her curls and looking earnest. "You're unattached — as far as we know — and eligible. Your father is a living doll; Mrs. Hunt, the world's Ninth Wonder; and you're probably going to be famous — although how your image emerges from a small town — ''

"Ah!" Andrew said. "Most images have, and do. Try to remember, Maggie, a place like this is a microcosm."

"She doesn't dig heavy words," Matt remarked.

"I do that one," Maggie said indignantly. "Also, Moxie likes me, which should put me high on your list, Matt."

"Lani cataloged all this?"

"Oh, no. I did. But don't fret. I may be *femme* but *femme fatale* I'm not, nor can I imagine following Lani's suggestion."

Matt shook his head. "You see," he said, and looked from his father to Mrs. Hunt, "you've both spoiled me; Maggie isn't interested because she isn't sorry for me."

"What has that to do with it?" Andrew asked.

Mrs. Hunt dropped a stitch and said plaintively, "How you two do run on."

"I am older than Maggie," Matt remarked. "Also wiser; also a damned sight more sensible."

"I'm glad to hear it," Andrew told him. "There are times when I think you believe you're still at the university. Even still in

288

high school."

"They do say we are adolescent until we're twenty-five," Maggie commented.

"Which clears me," Matt told her, "but not you, Junior Miz."

After a moment, Maggie said, "Wouldn't that make a marvelous mystery-novel title?"

Andrew and Mrs. Hunt looked at her bewildered. But Matt asked her gently, "How far ahead — or behind — in the conversation are you, Maggie?"

"Behind. It just struck me. The Cat in the Linen Closet. I must call Vanessa and tell her. She dotes on mysteries. I do too."

Early in the blaze of October, the Carstairs had returned. Maggie and Matt went to dinner one evening. There were perhaps half a dozen others. Lily and Alan looked brown and rested after Copenhagen and Switzerland. They'd traveled when, and as, they pleased. They were, however, glad to be home, they said. And when Maggie was leaving, Lily drew her aside. "There's nothing I can say," she told her quietly, "except thank you, Maggie."

On the way home, Matt said, "So you

needn't be sorry for Alan anymore."

"I believe not," Maggie answered. "But I don't know why — "

"You had merely to look at them, Maggie. Lily's as happy as she ever can be and he's happy as he was. Oh, I don't mean he won't grieve over Kim. But Kim was not his world's center."

November came and the elections. Maggie went early to vote. She had worked at the makeshift headquarters, evenings for the most part, sending out reminders, doing a great deal of telephoning, and on Election Night was at headquarters with Matt and the other men and women of his party.

They didn't all lose as it was not the usual clean sweep, but Matt did.

On the way back to the Comstock house for a post mortem, as Matt called it, Maggie said, "I'm so sorry."

"For me? Don't tell me."

"Well no," she said slightly surprised, "not for you personally because you don't seem disappointed."

"Oh, I'm disappointed all right. But I've

the satisfaction of knowing that I worked my tail off and made a few converts. I include you."

"You needn't. I voted for you because I know you; you and your father are my friends. But I honestly don't know enough about the town yet — and very little about your opponents — to form a considered opinion," she admitted.

"I'll instruct you," he told her. "You're really a very refreshing gal, Magpie. You tell the truth quite often. In this case because, one, you aren't sorry for me and two, as you aren't, I don't attract you. If you'd been in love with me," he added thoughtfully, "you would have voted for me, even if you'd studied the entire situation and believed I was the worst menace to be born in Little Oxford, also corrupt, destructive, and a bastard generally."

Maggie laughed. "Are you?"

"My mother preserved her marriage lines."

"I mean the rest."

"Hell, no."

At the Comstock house, Andrew, who

hadn't been at headquarters, said, "Thanks for the phone call."

"No news to you, I suppose?"

"I'm afraid not. Sorry I wasn't with you."

"How's the indigestion?"

"All right. How about a drink? Mrs. Hunt has sandwiches. You must both be tired."

"Home they brought her warrior dead," Matt remarked. "We sure had a turnout. The opposition was dancing in the streets, or some of them anyway. I've never seen that before here — "

"They've never come as close to losing before," his father said, "although still in the majority."

It was late when Matt took Maggie home and in the living room, with Moxie beside him, he said, "Thanks, Maggie, for everything." He kissed her and went off whistling "Tie a Yellow Ribbon."

Maggie collapsed into a chair and looked after him. In a few minutes she'd pull herself together, lock up, and go to bed. Tomorrow was a working day. It had been exciting, she thought, more than she'd believed possible. She'd enjoyed the glimpse she'd had into the workings of town politics. She would have to learn more. What had Andrew said . . . that a place like this one was a microcosm? It could teach you about larger towns, cities, states, the nation and the issues.

Thanksgiving she was at the Comstocks', and by then had her plane tickets to the Islands. She'd go out a week before the wedding and return right after the New Year. The hospital had given her the vacation; she'd been there a year.

"You'll never get one in summer now," Matt warned.

"Who cares? In ten years I'll have longer ones."

"We'll miss you," his father said.

"A repeat," said Matt, "every year, of course. Even I, in due time, will have to think about my future and look for a very rich widow. But we'll invite you both for Thanksgiving," he told Maggie and his father graciously, "as, of course, Mrs. Hunt will be with us."

"Not with you, young man," said Mrs. Hunt, passing the cranberry sauce. "I know when I'm well off."

"She'll never leave Micawber," Matt said sadly.

As he was taking Maggie home, she asked, "Aren't you ever serious?"

"Certainly. In court, in the judges' chambers, in the office. Moxie can testify to that."

"I wish things had gone better for you, Matt, in the election."

"They will next time," he assured her. "Wait and see."

"Your father looked tired tonight. He didn't do justice to Mrs. Hunt's dinner."

"He's been having a little gastric trouble. I'll get him to Bing as soon as I can break down his defenses. He has his own remedies of course — and takes them. He's been working hard and it's some time since he's had a checkup, though both Bing and Ben keep after him. It worries me, but if he sees I'm worried, he's enraged."

She said, "I think you hide a lot of — well — emotion. I just realized it."

"Well, thanks, Doctor. Shall we set up

my next session?''

"You're hopeless!''

"Wrong! I'm the most sanguine man you'll ever meet.''

"That's a switch! Before the election you predicted you'd lose.''

"Because I knew I would. Face up to it, bite on the bullet, I always say. What do you always say?''

"On this occasion, thank you and good night.''

"You're welcome. Planning a festive weekend for what's left of it?''

"Just lunch, dinner, shopping. I'll see Amy and possibly Ben for dinner Sunday. You're going away, I suppose?''

"Nope. Shall sulk in my tent. Good night, Magpie. Thanks for coming today.''

18

Ben came home late for dinner — "I never apologize for him," Amy said unnecessarily — and just before dessert. He said resignedly, "Hell's bells," and went to answer the telephone.

"I'll be right there," they heard him say.

He came back to stand briefly in the doorway. "Andrew Comstock," he said. "That was Matt. Call the ambulance, Amy. Have it meet me at the Comstocks'."

Maggie got to her feet as he tore out of the house; Amy was already at the phone.

When Amy came back, Maggie said, "I remember at Thanksgiving he complained of indigestion — but I didn't think it would be so serious."

Amy said, "There's nothing we can do, Maggie, except sit tight."

"I could call Mrs. Hunt — no, course not," Maggie sat down and looked at the bright chrysanthemums on the table; she had brought them. She said, "I can't bear to think it might be serious. He's been so good to me, Amy." Tears spilled over and ran down her cheeks and she said, "Excuse me," leaned down and groped in her handbag which was beside her chair.

"Here's a tissue," said Amy. "How about dessert?"

"No, thanks. I'm not hungry . . . I don't know whether to go home and wait until I think it's safe to call Mrs. Hunt or to stay here and wait for Ben."

"Go home, " Amy advised. "You'll feel better there. Ben may call me and he may not. Bing will be there, of course, and, if necessary, consultants."

"How come you always know what to say and do?"

"It took time to learn," Amy said. She put her arms around the younger woman and kissed her. "Drive carefully," she warned, "and if you want to talk, call me. I know how much you care for Andrew Comstock. All of us who know him are in the same boat."

Maggie drove home and left the car out. Mrs. Hunt, who didn't drive, might want to be taken somewhere. She let herself in the house, grateful for the dim lamp she'd left burning.

Matt knew, she thought. He was worried; that's why he didn't go away.

When the telephone rang, she ran to it. "Matt?" she asked, but it was Mrs. Hunt.

"Martha Hunt. . . . Matt asked me to call you. His father's been taken very sick. He's gone by ambulance to the hospital. Dr. Ben was here . . . Matt's to call me. He said to let you know and we'd keep in touch."

"What was it?" asked Maggie, "or don't you know?"

"Heart. They took him to emergency, and then to Intensive Care. Matt said no use my going up. Only members of families are allowed in Intensive Care — and then only for a few mintues." Her voice roughened. "Queer," she added. "All these years I've felt I *was* family."

"You are, Maggie said. "Of course you are."

"Well, a rule's a rule. I'll call when I

know anything. I'm to call Mrs. Daniels now; she'll notify everyone at the office."

Maggie heard nothing further that night and didn't, in consequence, sleep much of it. She was up early, in the kitchen drinking coffee and listening for the telephone when Matt walked in. "Save me a cup," he suggested.

Maggie ran to put her arms about him. "Oh, Matt," she said, "I'm sorry, so sorry . . . "

He held her and patted her back. "Brace up," he said. "Here, sit down." He looked as if he'd been through a private war. "The medical boys think Dad'll be all right. Bing, Ben and a pride of specialists. I dunno of course how long he's to be in ICU before they transfer him, or how long in the hospital thereafter. He'll make it, Maggie. Don't fret; just pray."

When she reached the hospital, somewhat late, everyone on the staff apparently had heard "rumors and counter-rumors," Mr. Davis said, "but as far as we know he's doing well."

"He'd better," Mrs. Cromwell said. He was the Cromwells' family lawyer and

299

also their friend.

"Now," said Mr. Davis briskly, "there's a certain amount of work to be accomplished and Andrew wouldn't appreciate it if we just sat here and looked apprehensive."

It was a couple of weeks before Maggie saw Andrew Comstock. He had had round-the-clock nurses when he was moved from ICU to a private room, but now there was just one, a Mrs. Thomas, round, rosy, and extremely competent. The room was on a corner, bright with December sunshine — there'd been no snow as yet — and flowers. Maggie had brought magazines for which he thanked her.

"I think Mrs. Hunt was scandalized," she admitted, sitting beside him, "but I figured you'd have enough flowers."

"The medical boys wouldn't let me have any for quite a spell," he told her, "and when they relaxed the edict, the place looked like a high-class funeral parlor. Now don't say, 'Don't talk like that.' "

"I wasn't going to, Mr. C."

She'd called him that for some time

when it wasn't Mr. Comstock.

"Unbend," said Andrew, "couldn't you bring youself to say, Andy; or if not, Uncle?"

He looked well, Maggie thought. His color was good, his eyes bright, but he had lost considerable weight.

"I don't want to tire you, Uncle Andrew."

"You haven't yet. Mrs. Thomas has left for the day, so I'll be the one to throw you out. Stay around. Matt will be coming by."

"I'd better go. It's your suppertime."

"Sorry you can't share it with me. It isn't as bad as most patients insist; that's a fixation. Of course Mrs. Thomas is around at breakfast and lunch and she also orders my supper, so I'm greatly pampered."

"I've been terribly worried," Maggie said. "And I'm so glad to see you well."

"Well, thanks, dear. . . . Hi, Matt."

"Look who's here," said Matt, "as if I didn't know you would be."

Maggie rose. She said, "One at a time, I think."

"That's right. Wait for me in the coffee

shop. I'll buy supper."

So she waited, having found a corner table and ordered coffee in order to hold it. "I'm waiting," she told the volunteer, "for a friend."

"Matt?" said the volunteer. "How's his father? I haven't heard today."

"Doing fine," said Maggie mechanically. She thought: Everyone in this hospital knows everything.

Then he came.

"How is he, really?" Maggie asked.

"Could outlive us both," Matt said, "if he takes care of himself, and between Mrs. Hunt, Mrs. Daniels, you and me, he will. Of course he hates to be told what to do at any time as his life work consists of telling other people what to do — including, after his fashion — juries. I'm sorry I can't go to Lani's wedding with you, Magpie."

Maggie just looked at him.

You look like a fish with curly red hair. Close your mouth," he said.

"You really intended to go? I can't believe it."

"Believe it. I was going to take a few days off."

"But why?"

"I wanted to meet the rest of your family and besides since watching 'Hawaii-Five-O,' I've longed to go the aloha route. At one time I thought about a double wedding but it wasn't logical; too much to arrange in a hurry."

"Matt," she asked seriously, "don't you feel well?"

"I'm in excellent health," he said with dignity. "Let's eat supper. I'll go up and see Dad again afterwards for a few minutes and then follow you home. We can discuss this over a beaker of something or other."

Before he came, Maggie sat down in an armchair and put her feet on a hassock. She thought: This isn't happening. It can't be.

When Matt arrived he made himself a drink. "You'd better have one," he told her, "light but soothing."

"No thanks."

"Why so withdrawn? You are perceptibly shrinking; you can't afford that. Oh, I see. Last time I mentioned the risky institution of marriage — and some people think Wall Street has ups and downs — was, if my memory serves me, after we'd seen Lani off and I'd taken you to the partly singles' bar. You said then I was off my rocker.''

''But you can't be serious,'' Maggie said.

''I'm serious. We've known each other somewhat over a year and I made up my mind early. Why I don't know, as actually you're not my type. Now you can just fly off to Hawaii and make up your mind. Lani might help.''

''Matt — ''

''Oh, I told her. I need a friend.''

She said, ''I like you more than any man I've ever known. I'm very fond of you — but in love?'' She shook her head.

''Who said anything about love?''

She was scarlet, got to her feet and asked furiously, ''You don't love me?''

''Of course. I just asked who said anything about it?''

He was laughing at her and she said, ''I could kill you.''

''That's a good start,'' he told her. ''I'll take you to the plane, Maggie. We'll argue all the way." He leaned down, took her in his arms and kissed her. "Do think about it, Magpie," he said.

She thought about it. Now and then she saw him, and Moxie often came by. Matt said nothing further, however, except once, gravely, "We have Moxie's approval, which is remarkable when you come to think of it." Later he said, "You know I'd go with you to Hawaii, but I have to look after my senior partner. Fortunately, there's the room and bath off the library but, even so, he's a handful."

That evening Maggie thought: He looks older . . . and realized that he had since his father's illness; and there were lines in his face which she'd never noticed before. She thought: He worries all the time, but I can't be sorry for him. He can take it.

He was not a leaner. Every man in whom she'd been interested was.

"Don't forget to come back," Andrew said the day before her flight.

"How could I?"

"Easily," he told her smiling. "Home town, familiar surroundings, your family."

"There's that," Maggie agreed, "but I'm beginning to feel I belong here."

"Give her a couple more years," Matt said, "and she'll no longer be our new girl in town."

At the airport, in the waiting room of her airline, he sat beside her in a bright red chair and said, "You'll come back?"

"Yes."

"To me?"

She smiled at him, on that dark day with a few flakes drifting down and nervous passengers looking out.

"I don't know . . . I don't quite know."

"I wonder," he said thoughtfully, "if electric guitars, moonlight on the Pacific and long white beaches would help."

"I doubt it."

"Maggie" — he took her hand and held it — "give my love to Lani, my respects to Greg. I'll phone before Christmas. And I'll save all festivities until you come home."

Her flight was called and he walked to the gate with her, then pulled her into his arms. He said, "If you don't make up your mind my way, you'll simply fall violently in love with me."

"Come again?"

"You'll be so sorry for me," Matt said triumphantly. "I'm sure you could never resist a discarded lover."

"You're absolutely right," Maggie said. "I've just been checked through Security before departing and I'm pretty sure I'll return to it." She stood on tiptoe and kissed him. "When I get back," she promised, "we'll learn to know each other."

He stood, his hands in his pockets, and watched her go — small, erect, his little love. He was smiling.